GOLEM 4
MR WILLIAM

The Murail siblings are all hugely successful authors in their own right – Marie-Aude has sold over two million books worldwide, Elvire's very first novel was turned into a film and Lorris is well known for writing about his two passions: good food and science fiction. Together they make a truly formidable literary trio. When writing the Golem series, the siblings wanted not only to recapture the intensity and creativity of playing together as children, but also to write the kinds of books they would have liked when they were young. "It was like a game," says Elvire, the youngest. "It was a huge challenge, but we wanted to lose our individual voices and morph into a new, even better one. It worked so well that sometimes we had trouble remembering who had written what!" Her sister Marie-Aude adds, "It's so important to remember what you were like when you were young. It gets more difficult as you get older – you have to have your own children to get it back again!" It took two years to complete all five Golem books.

Now it is your turn to play...

This book is supported by the French
Ministry for Foreign Affairs, as part of
the Burgess programme headed for
the French Embassy in London by the
Institut Français du Royaume-Uni

Liberté • Égalité • Fraternité
RÉPUBLIQUE FRANÇAISE

Golem
4: Mr William

Elvire, Lorris and Marie-Aude Murail
translated by Sarah Adams

WALKER BOOKS
AND SUBSIDIARIES

LONDON • BOSTON • SYDNEY • AUCKLAND

First published 2005 by Walker Books Ltd
87 Vauxhall Walk, London SE11 5HJ

2 4 6 8 10 9 7 5 3 1

Original Edition: *Golem 4 – Monsieur William*
© 2002 Éditions Pocket Jeunesse,
a division of Univers Poche, Paris – France
Translation © 2005 Sarah Adams
Cover image © 2005 Guy McKinley

The right of Elvire, Lorris and Marie-Aude Murail to be
identified as authors of this work has been asserted by them
in accordance with the Copyright, Designs and Patents Act 1988

This book has been typeset in DeadHistory and M Joanna

Printed and bound in Great Britain
by Bookmarque Ltd, Croydon, Surrey

British Library Cataloguing in Publication Data:
a catalogue record for this book
is available from the British Library

ISBN 1-84428-617-7

www.walkerbooks.co.uk

Contents

0%
10%
20%
30%
40%
50%
60
70%
80%
90

In Golem: LEVEL 3:

There's no doubt about it, virtual reality's getting a lot more real. Characters keep on escaping from the pirate computer game that has taken Moreland Town by storm. First there was Joke, the blob-shaped golem in the basements. Next came Bubble the dragon, and now Natasha, teacher Hugh's virtual girlfriend. Natasha has only two lives left in which to win her soul and complete her mission: to destroy the multinational company B Corp. She's helped by her creator, Hugh; computer whizz Albert; and science teacher Nadia. So far they have avoided the traps set by B Corp to lure them back to its Swiss HQ, but for how long can they keep one step ahead?

... 100%

››Transfer complete

START PLAY ››

Class Progress Meeting

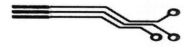

For tiny Mrs Cure – Andrea by first name and maths teacher by job – a class progress meeting was an important event. It was where the futures of the "children", as she insisted on calling them (even when they wore size 13 trainers and had a criminal record), got decided.

Which was why Andrea Cure had been the first to arrive in the staffroom for 8D's progress meeting. She was bent over her register, analysing its contents. Sebastian had scored the highest term average. But her top student had underperformed recently and sometimes seemed distracted in class. Maybe his parents were having a bad time. Or was there a new little brother or sister in the picture? Mrs Cure doodled a question mark. She ran her biro up and down the list in search of the second highest mark, and drew a line under Samir Ben Azet. Who'd have thought it? He might have an attitude problem, but Samir also had real potential. Mrs Cure put an exclamation mark in the margin. She wanted to understand her students. As she reminded the head, Mr Moore, at least twenty times a year, it was important to know about their track record and family background. There was an explanation for everything, even the most alarming behaviour.

The sound of whispering in the corridor alerted her to the arrival of 8D's class representatives. "Come in, children!" she called.

"'Lo, Mrs Cure," mumbled Sebastian and Nouria, before shuffling over to their seats. They looked exhausted as they sat down next to each other, eyes to the floor.

"Is everything all right?" asked Mrs Cure.

Sebastian looked up blankly. Nouria had just told him what Aisha had seen near the Moreland Estate the previous evening. It took a good ten seconds for his teacher's question to sink in.

"Fine," he said at last.

Mrs Cure added another question mark beside his name, increasingly convinced his parents were going through a divorce.

Miss Berry, the history and geography teacher, walked in at this point, and turned bright red on seeing her colleague. "Am I late?"

"No, not at all. I'm early," Mrs Cure said reassuringly. But she couldn't help shaking her head. Poor Miss Berry! How could they get her to smarten herself up? She wasn't exactly ugly, but she slouched and let her hair flop over her face. Not like Nadia Martin, the stylish science teacher who was always sassily dressed.

No sooner had this thought crossed her mind than in walked Nadia. Mrs Cure stifled a gasp. She looked like she'd just tumbled out of bed. At quarter past five in the afternoon. Her hair was all over the place, her blouse was buttoned up wrong and her mascara had got smudged, giving her a couple of black eyes.

Nadia put a hand to her heaving chest. "Phew! I weally wan!" And with no further explanation, she collapsed onto a chair and put her head in her hands.

Mrs Cure ventured two guesses. One: Nadia had been out partying with her friends and, since she didn't teach on Tuesdays, she'd had a very long lie-in. Such behaviour wasn't entirely appropriate for a teacher, but it was excusable at her age. Two: Nadia had argued with her boyfriend and had been at the sleeping pills. A romantic at heart, Mrs Cure was inclined to believe the second and felt sorry for the pretty teacher who'd just been jilted. But Nadia, who was miles away, started laughing softly to herself. And staring into space. She was picturing Albert as she'd left him half an hour ago in their hotel room. Stark naked. Tanned, buff, fit, the cat that'd got the cream. She let out a sigh that sounded far from heartbroken.

Madame Dupond, the French teacher, turned up next.

"Afternoon all," she said in the rushed tone of voice she used when there was a lot to get through. "Is everybody here?" She frowned, already in a bad mood, and glanced at the clock. She had two small children and was steering a tricky course between earache and chickenpox. "Shall we get started?"

"Er, well," objected Mrs Cure, "we should really make sure that Mr Mu— Ah, here he is…"

Mrs Cure couldn't even bring herself to say hello to Hugh. She just gawped. After several sleepless nights, 8D's English teacher had finally nodded off with his head on the keyboard. He looked worse than exhausted. He was totally run-down. Bloodshot eyes, unruly hair, feverish cracked lips. Mrs Cure knew he'd been off work sick. Was he depressed? He appeared to be on another planet. Or on tranquillizers.

"Right, are we ready?" asked Madame Dupond, interrupting Mrs Cure's train of thought. "Let's start with…" – she smiled at 8D's male class representative – "congratulations, Sebastian!"

"Ah, Sebastian!" exclaimed Hugh, as if he'd only just realized his student was there. "What've you done with Joke? Is he still in the basements?"

Sebastian glanced anxiously at the assembled faces. Was Hugh going to talk about the electric ectoplasm in front of everybody? "No," he replied. "We've put him in the old quarry."

"You can talk about what you've got to move and where later on," cut in Madame Dupond impatiently. "Right, Sebastian, we're satisfied you're ready for Year 9, and well done again. Samir Ben Azet?"

Nadia twitched and seemed to shake herself out of her dream world. "Ah, yes, Thamir!"

It was because of Samir that her life had been turned upside down.

"How did Thamir get hold of a BIT mobile phone from B Corp?" she asked out loud.

Hugh's eyes nearly popped out of his head. "B Corp? B Corp must be destroyed," he chanted in a robotic voice.

"That's what Albert thinks," said Nadia.

"You know Albert?"

"Of course I do. I've shared a be— I mean, had dinner with him wecently!" Nadia turned bright red. If she didn't watch out, she'd put her foot in it.

"We *are* here for the progress meeting, aren't we?" asked Miss Berry, always quick to assume she'd got the wrong time or the wrong day or the wrong meeting.

"Of course we are," said Madame Dupond, trying to pick up the pace. "Right, Ben Azet. Are we satisfied he's ready for Year 9? Clearly, there have been a few discipline problems."

"But it's not his fault," Sebastian objected. "He's got to look after his sister, Lulu, who's sick, and his parents drink…"

"Gracious me," whispered Mrs Cure, scribbling *alcoholic parents* in her register.

"And on top of that he's got to make sure Joke gets fed properly," added Sebastian, looking to Hugh for back-up.

"Is that his little brother?" guessed Miss Berry.

Sebastian pictured the giant white monster hiding in the quarry. "Not … exactly," he muttered, hoping Hugh would come to his rescue.

"Not at all," the young teacher corrected him. "Joke is a golem." He looked at everybody sitting around the table. "You *do* all know what a golem is, don't you?" he asked, starting to lose his temper.

There was a thoughtful silence. Mrs Cure wondered if Mr Mullins wouldn't perhaps benefit from extending his sick leave.

"We haven't discussed Majid yet, have we?" Hugh wanted to know. He'd only turned up to make sure the youngest Badach didn't have to stay down a year.

"No, we've got as far as Aisha," said Madame Dupond firmly. "Right, Aisha. I think she needs to stay down, don't you?"

"She's got 2 in algebra," said Mrs Cure, under-lining the mark with her biro, "and 1 in geometry. Her marks have slipped this term."

"But it's not her fault!" whined Nouria, Aisha's best friend.

"She's got an overprotective father, if I remem-ber correctly," sympathized Mrs Cure.

"It ain't that! It's coz of the dead spirits that keep chasing her. She even saw them in the street yesterday evening. They've got claws and teeth and … um … er … fur."

Descriptions had never been Nouria's strong point, but her English teacher recognized the holo-grams that had escaped from his computer.

"The Evildoers!" he exclaimed. "They escaped from my flat. Aisha saw them?"

"Yes, sir, got the shock of her life, sir."

Mrs Cure had heard about the Mean Sharks, a crew that terrorized certain areas of Moreland

Town. But she wasn't familiar with the Evildoers. "Listen, Nouria, if these Evildoers are bullying Aisha, she must tell her father about it."

"But he's gonna disbelieve her, innit?" said Nouria indignantly. "I were disbelievin' her too, to start with."

Madame Dupond seized the chance to settle matters. "Nouria, given your difficulties grasping basic grammar, I think the best thing would be if you stayed down as well. How about repeating the year together?"

"The whole class'll be staying down at this rate!" objected Hugh. "In any case, when it comes to Majid, I'm totally against the idea."

Mrs Cure's biro was now poised under the name of Badach. "I'd just like to point out that he only got 1 this term in algeb—"

"But it's not his fault!" interrupted Sebastian. "The test was on a Monday and Majid had to look after Joke all weekend. So he couldn't revise."

"Aha, so Joke's *Majid's* little brother," said Miss Berry, relieved she'd understood something at last.

"He's a *golem*!" Hugh ticked her off. "Are you making *any* effort to follow this discussion?"

"A golem like the one in the game?" wondered Nadia.

"A golem out of the computer game Golem, yes," said Hugh, becoming increasingly irritated.

"*Albert's* computer game?"

"What is it with you and Albert?"

"Nothing," lied Nadia brazenly. "Anyway, you're the one Albert wants to see."

"Suits me," Hugh smirked. "I've got a few things to run by him, because, guess what, his computer game keeps coming out of my PC in detachable pieces."

"This is the class progress meeting, isn't it?" sighed Miss Berry.

"Of course it is," growled Madame Dupond. "But if we keep talking about computer games, we'll never get to the end of it. Right, OK, Majid Badach. Scrapes into Year 9, is that what we're saying?"

"Hold on! He only got 1 in geometry this term," said Mrs Cure, pointing to the mark in her register.

Hugh continued his conversation with Nadia. "Where is Albert?"

"In…" Nadia pictured the seedy hotel room again. "I'm not allowed to say."

"But I've got to talk to him," he pleaded. "We're running out of time."

"You're telling me," said Madame Dupond. "Right, Mamadou… What have his marks been like in English?"

"Now look here, Madame Dupond," said Hugh, trying to speak calmly. "I can make characters from a computer game escape from my PC, and there's a dragon living in a cage in my flat. He's not very big, I'll grant you that, but he's a nuisance and I'd like to discuss the problem with the game's inventor."

"Is this the meeting for the end of year play?" Miss Berry was feeling increasingly miserable.

Mrs Cure noted *schizophrenia?* in her register. She should alert the head at once.

"Sir? Did you *really* make the dragon come out of your computer?" Sebastian whistled.

"Yes – in a scaled-down version." Hugh's hands measured out twenty centimetres.

"I don't believe this! We're not going to spend the entire meeting talking about computer games!"

Madame Dupond was choking with indignation. Single men these days! They clearly had nothing better to do than talk about themselves. "My little Jasper is teething at the moment, and he's got a temperature of a hundred and one!"

Mrs Cure gave Madame Dupond a pitying look. Didn't she realize Mr Mullins had gone mad? "Hugh," she said as kindly as possible, "I'm sure you can sort things out with your dragon later."

"But there's Natasha too," he objected. "I'm not letting her back out of my computer for the time being, because she's dangerous." He immediately qualified this statement. "I don't mean deliberately dangerous. But she's virtual. She just fires her eraser-laser without realizing it can kill." And to prove his point, he added, "Each time she shoots, she thinks she'll score bonus points."

"Of course she does," agreed Mrs Cure.

Meanwhile, Madame Dupond was gathering her belongings and telling Miss Berry that her child-minder had rung to say she was locked out because her daughter, Jasmine, had managed to lose the keys, and if she didn't pick up Jasper's medical records before seven o'clock this evening she wouldn't be able to see the paediatrician recommended by her sister for children with chronic earache.

"Oh, really? Well, gosh!" stammered Miss Berry, keen to look like she was involved in the meeting at some level.

Nadia was listening to Hugh with growing astonishment. Albert had told her about the subliminal imaging he'd slipped into his game. But Hugh was talking about something totally different.

"What's all this about a dwagon in a cage?" she lisped. "Are you making it up, or what?"

"Shh," whispered Mrs Cure, "shh." When somebody was suffering from delusions, they needed careful handling.

"He's definitely not making it up," cut in Sebastian. "We've got a golem too."

"Not you as well, Sebastian," Mrs Cure said despairingly. "If your parents aren't getting on at the moment, just tell yourself it's a bad patch but they'll work it out in the end."

"My parents are cool," Sebastian reassured her. "And the golem's fine too. We've hidden him in the quarry."

"The quarry?" echoed Nadia. She was starting to see a solution to her problem. "Albert and I have got B Corp after us," she told Hugh, "and we're looking for a hideout. Why not the quarry?"

The more dramatic the news, the better its chance of reaching Hugh's brain. So the idea that Nadia was also being chased by killers from B Corp didn't faze him in the slightest.

"I've got a better hideout," said Sebastian. "My parents' camper van. They only use it in the summer holidays."

Miss Berry thought she'd had a brainwave. "Is this the meeting for the end of year trip?"

Tiny Mrs Cure stood up shakily. She'd also just seen the light: farting goo. Everybody had tubs of Big B farting goo at Moreland School. They'd said on TV that it might contain a hallucinogenic substance. Nadia, Hugh and Sebastian had clearly all pummelled the goo and been brainwashed.

She rushed out into the corridor in search of the head. "Mr Moore! Mr Moore!"

By the time she'd finally tracked him down, she was beetroot, sweaty, dishevelled. She looked like a lunatic.

"Ah, Mr Moore, it's just dreadful!" she exclaimed. "Dreadful! Mr Mullins keeps seeing dragons everywhere – little dragons." Mrs Cure measured out twenty centimetres with her trembling hands. "And Nadia, Nadia Martin, you should see her – anybody'd think she'd spent the last fortnight clubbing. Even Sebastian – you remember him, Sebastian in 8D?"

"Yes, yes, yes," said Mr Moore soothingly, resting his hands on the tiny teacher's shoulders to calm her down.

"Well, he's hiding golems in some basements – no, a quarry ... or a camper van. It's just dreadful!"

"Dreadful!" agreed Mr Moore rather too emphatically.

There was an explanation for everything, thought the head, even the most alarming behaviour. Was Mrs Cure separating from her husband? Or had she started drinking?

Who Doesn't Like Kids?

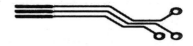

Albert was feeling mellow. Sprawled across the unmade bed, he was blowing smoke rings at the ceiling. He was mellow, but there was nothing in his pocket. Then again, he thought, I don't really need pockets any more. He was naked. Just as Nadia had left him an hour ago. He let out a contented sigh. That babe was really, really...

"Gorgeous!" he told the light above his head.

He was answered by the door. *Knock-knock.*

"Whoops!" he exclaimed, grabbing his boxers. "Who is it?"

"Puss in Boots," replied the person on the other side.

Albert pushed the door open a fraction and saw Granter standing on the landing.

"Is that all B Corp left you with?" said his former colleague as he walked in.

"Just the skin on my back," confirmed Albert. "Shut the door. Are you sure nobody followed you?"

Granter shrugged and put his laptop down on the bed.

Albert cut straight to the point. "So, B Corp wants to get rid of you too?"

Granter nodded.

"What did you do wrong?"

"I left before I was fired. D'you know what firing somebody means at B Corp?" Granter's eyes darted about as he talked. He didn't trust anybody.

"Are you paranoid or what?" Albert said. "OK, I'll put my cards on the table."

He gestured around the seedy hotel room, his last refuge. "I haven't got much choice. It's this or the Salvation Army, and I don't think my girlfriend would be into that."

"Who?"

"My girlfriend."

Granter scowled. He was short, fat and bald. Albert got on his nerves, fancying himself as a computer wizard, when actually he was just a slimy con artist. He sat on the bed and powered up his laptop. The computer was the only "person" he really talked to.

"You know I was working on Golem while I was at Gruyères?" Albert carried on. "It was a ... peculiar job. Our favourite boss, Mr William, wanted to give his young customers the chance to experience mental manipulation at first hand. I was asked to insert a subliminal message into my animated sequences. Just a funny gag: Buy Big B farting goo!"

Granter was typing rapidly. "And ... did you ... do what you were asked?" he said slowly.

"Yes."

Silence. Granter typed: I thought as much. The guy's a crook. Then he pressed delete. "Did it pay well?" he asked levelly.

"Yeah, big money. But I walked away from it in the end."

"Guilty conscience?" Granter said sarcastically.

"There was some dodgy business going on.

The more I worked on Golem, the more I got the feeling somebody was programming in data behind my back. The game … how can I put this? The game was getting away from me. I suspected saboteurs in my team. And I wondered if they were acting on Mr William's orders."

Granter typed: I thought the same thing. Then he came to a decision. "OK. I'll show my cards now. Mr William hired me because I'm the leading expert in security systems…" He paused and wrote: in the world but finished off more modestly: "In Europe."

"That didn't stop your system crashing on us," Albert pointed out.

Slimy con artist! Granter let rip on the screen. Then he carried on calmly. "I ran into endless problems trying to install Artificial Logical Intelligence for Absolute Security. I got the feeling Mr William was sabotaging the work behind my back too."

"Why? Was he looking for flaws in the system?"

Granter wrote: My security system is rock solid. But since I had to introduce it into ALL the computerized systems at HQ, maybe there was some kind of interference between the programs?????????????????????

The truth was he'd been totally flummoxed. And he'd been scared of being accused of sabotage himself. So he'd got out.

There was another knock at the door. Albert and Granter were both nervous wrecks and nearly jumped off the bed.

"Who is it?" called Albert.

Nadia gave her code name: "Little Wed Widing Hood."

Albert winked at Granter as he got up to open the door. "My life's a fairy tale come true."

Nadia walked in and gasped when she saw a stranger sitting on the bed.

Albert introduced his ex-colleague. "This is Granter. I've managed to get my hands on him at last. And this," he said to Granter, "is my girlfriend."

Granter snapped his laptop shut. He didn't get on with women. "You've caught up with me, but you won't be able to contact me again," he announced hastily. "I'm leaving the country. My new company's sending me … somewhere far away. But I want to tell you something before I go." He was just talking to Albert now.

"Hoax," he said, getting up.

"Hoax," repeated Albert.

"What kind of hoax?" asked Nadia.

Brushing her aside with a wave of his hand, Granter went on. "B Corp is a colossal enterprise. But even a multinational has its weak points. You've heard about the tubs of goo that are meant to be hallucinogenic?"

Nadia and Albert looked at each other. So there *was* some truth in the rumour after all.

"Hoax," said Granter again. "And I started it."

He headed for the door. "I'm leaving you the laptop. You should be able to do some damage with your subliminal messaging info."

Nadia waited until the door was closed before saying, "What a weird guy! And have you vowed never to get dwessed again or something?" She couldn't get used to the idea that this hunk was her boyfriend, and felt herself blushing.

Albert's heart melted. He grabbed her, hugging her close. "You know I'm crazy about you?" Then he laughed, as if his remark had caught him by surprise, and let her go. He sat down cross-legged on the bed. "A New Generation BIT laptop," he whispered tenderly, stroking the lid before opening it.

A few flurries with his fingers and then he whistled. "Take a look at this guy's address book!"

It didn't take Albert long to explain about hoaxes and pyramid emails. They were rumours started on the Net by jokers or crooks. You got an email that began: *Forward this to as many people as possible! Don't eat bananas for the next three weeks!* The message went on to explain that bananas from Costa Rica were infected by necrotizing fasciitis, a notorious flesh-eating bacteria.

"So what we're saying is, eat that banana and you're the one who ends up getting munched," he explained with a winning smile.

"But it's just an urban myth," exclaimed Nadia.

"It's a hoax. If ten people fall for it and forward the email to another ten people, who fall for it and forward it as well, you get a snowball effect. One day the press are saying: 'There's a possibility of Costa Rican bananas being infected', and the next there's a major TV report: 'Panic on the streets. The banana strikes back!'"

"It's pathetic."

"But it works. Want proof? Granter started a

hoax about hallucinogenic farting goo and now everybody's talking about it."

Nadia scowled, still sceptical. "Not everybody believes it."

"*Not everybody* is still quite a lot," said Albert. "Look at Granter's address book."

He scrolled down it while Nadia watched. Hundreds and hundreds of email addresses. Chances were they were Internet freaks and computer analysts, just the right people to pass on top-notch scams. "And we're going to use them," murmured Albert. He thought for a moment before writing:

Hi everybody! Need to clean your toilet?
What's stopping you? Pour in a can of
Big B cola. Leave for an hour, then flush.
Sparkling clean! Big B cola contains
phosphoric acid, just like your favourite
brand of toilet descaler. And you let your
kids drink it?! Thanks, B Corp!

Nadia, who was reading over his shoulder, started laughing.

"Go forth and multiply…" he announced, sending the message to Granter's entire address book.

"But how does that help?"

"I'm going to spread the rumour that B Corp is a sect, Mr William thinks he's the new Messiah, children get kidnapped at B Happy Land to remove their kidneys—"

"But nobody'll believe a word of it!" scoffed Nadia.

"People'll end up believing it all, because I'm also going to tell them something that we can prove is true."

"Which is?"

Albert was looking very serious now.

"B Corp has inserted subliminal messaging into Golem."

Nadia wandered over to the window, leaving Albert glued to the screen. She tweaked the curtain to watch night falling. She was starting to second-guess his behaviour. He couldn't denounce B Corp's schemes to the police, because he was implicated. But thanks to the anonymity of the Net, he could still make a confession of sorts.

She walked back to the bed and stared at him so hard he couldn't help noticing. "It's all-out war," he declared. "Albert versus B Corp."

Nadia didn't say anything. She had a mind-boggling rumour to pass on too. But hers was true. *Beware! Golem has a habit of escaping from your computer.* Hugh had mentioned holograms. Was Albert responsible for this virtual takeover as well?

She leant over his shoulder again. He was typing frenziedly:

New offensive by mafia firm B Corp! First hallucinogenic farting goo, now Golem, the game that hijacks your PCs. The goal of B Corp and its boss, Mr William, is as simple as it is terrifying: to manipulate your children's subconscious. That's right, this game contains a subliminal message that can be detected in slow motion…

"The boffins in cyberspace will check it out," said Albert, sending the message. He knew his only chance of leading a normal life again was to beat B Corp. "Who's the smartest now?" he crowed.

Nadia stroked his hair distractedly. "I've found a hideout that won't cost anything," she said after a while.

"Aha! So you're *not* just a pretty face!"

She flicked his head lightly. "And I've given my key to Thugh so he can pick up some clothes for me."

Albert glanced up. He didn't like hearing Hugh's name on Nadia's lips. "Weren't you in love with him?" he asked grudgingly.

"With who? Thugh?"

"Yeah, Thingy!"

Nadia laughed. Anger flashed in Albert's brooding eyes. But he forced a smile. "So where's your hidey-hole, darling?"

"It's a camper van, honey."

"Thingy's camper van?"

"No, it belongs to one of my students. Sebathian."

"Well, he'd better keep away," muttered Albert. "This isn't a kids' story."

But the following morning Sebastian was standing with Hugh at the entrance to the caravan park, behind the station.

"What's all this?" Sebastian asked.

Hugh had put a heavy suitcase down on the ground, but he was still clutching a wooden crate with airholes, tied up with a lot of string. "Clothes for Nadia."

Sebastian looked at the box and wondered what sort of clothes needed to breathe. Hugh checked his knots were secure again, then gave the crate a gentle shake. He seemed preoccupied.

"What's *really* inside?" asked Sebastian.

Just then Nadia and Albert appeared, walking briskly from the station. They were terrified of being spotted by Eddie, the contract killer from B Corp, in his white van.

"Thingy's here," murmured Albert. "But why'd he drag the kid along too?"

"Don't you like childwen?" Nadia flared. "I want three of them."

Albert slipped her a worried look.

The handshake between Hugh and Albert was manly and serious.

"Hello."

"Hi."

Sebastian led them down rows of parked vehicles, singing the praises of his family's camper van. "There's a shower and a toilet and two seats that turn into beds. Personally, I prefer the double bed above the front seats. You climb up a small ladder, and it feels like a bed in a boat if you push the curtains across—"

"Tell you what, how about you push off?" Albert butted in.

Nadia gave him a shocked look. But Albert pulled such a big kid's face she couldn't help smiling.

Inside the camper van, she opened cupboards and drawers and tried the double bed for comfort. Embarrassed, Hugh went outside again, and Sebastian followed.

"Albert's right for once," Hugh told him. "You'd better not hang around. Go on, hop it!"

Sebastian nodded and pretended to do as he was told. Then he turned and jerked his head towards the crate his teacher was still clutching. "What is it?"

"A surprise for Albert."

Sebastian took one step, before turning round once more and whispering, "So it's true, then?"

Hugh shrugged. "Yes, but in miniature."

"Thugh!" called Nadia.

Hugh went back inside. Albert was stretched out on one of the window seats, smoking.

"Thanks for the suitcase," said Nadia. "You even

wemembered my make-up. I weally appweciate it."

Hugh smiled at her sadly, as if he suddenly realized he'd missed out. Virtual girlfriends were all very well. But you couldn't show them off like Albert was doing with Nadia.

He put the crate down on the table and felt better. He didn't want to share his secret, but he knew he'd crack up if he kept it to himself. "Albert, I've got to talk to you."

The big hunk leant on his elbow and gave the wimpy teacher a condescending look.

"Did you program the characters in Golem to escape from the computer?"

"Come again?"

Hugh took a deep breath and repeated his question. "Did you program the game so that Natasha, Joke, the Evildoers and Bubble could escape from the computer?"

Albert glanced at Nadia. "How well d'you know this guy?"

"I think you need to explain yourself a bit more clearly, Thugh," she said.

"There's nothing to explain. Joke's in the quarry, guzzling electricity. Natasha's inside my computer, but I know how to get her out. The Evildoers were out, but they must have exploded in the rain…"

Albert looked at Nadia again. "Are there a lot of teachers like this?"

Nadia didn't know what to think any more. She let out a despairing sigh. Then, curious, she watched Hugh untying the string around the crate.

"I had a feeling you wouldn't believe me," he said, "so I've brought Bubble. That way you can see for yourselves."

Albert sat up like a shot. Nadia leant over the crate.

Hugh savoured the moment. "So I'm a nutcase?"

No answer.

"There's no dragon inside? No scaled-down Bubble who spits fire and gives you electric shocks, hey?"

"Thugh," begged Nadia.

Slowly, ever so slowly, the young teacher opened the lid. Just a crack. There was Bubble, shy and huddled. The journey must have shaken him up. He didn't move, but stayed pressed against one of the walls.

"He's so cute!" exclaimed Nadia.

"Is it … a tie-in product?" stammered Albert. "B Corp must have brought out plastic drago— Wow, it moved! It just moved then, didn't it?"

"What d'you reckon?" Hugh asked him calmly.

"Does it use batteries? Is it a kind of … what d'you call it … Furby?"

"What d'you reckon?" Hugh asked again.

The little dragon raised his muzzle. His blue eyes had turned red.

"Watch out," warned Hugh.

Suddenly Bubble spat his jet of fire as far as he could. Hugh closed the lid. Then, with a haunted look in his eyes, he blurted, "And I've got a girl with an eraser-laser back at my place. She's killed my goldfish and burnt my heart. I even kissed her and it hurt because she's electric. She wants to destroy B Corp. That's her mission, but water makes her disconnect and she's only got two lives left. And I love her…" His eyes were brimming with tears.

Albert lifted the lid again and moved his hand towards Bubble. Then he pulled it back, shouting, "Pile of junk! It burns!" He shut the lid again roughly.

Hugh was still crying, but he'd started laughing too. "So what d'you reckon – am I a nutcase?" he asked, on the brink of turning into one.

Lulu Flips

Lulu was bouncing around her bedroom, straddling a ball almost as tall as she was.

"See," said Mrs Ben Azet. "She's been like this for days now. All day long she's at it, all night too. I keep yelling at her to stop."

His bottom perched on the edge of Lulu's bed, Dr Andreas mopped his brow. "If I hadn't seen what she was like before, I know what I'd say…"

"What would you say?" asked Samir. He was leaning against the door frame, his legs wobbly and his brain pulp. Lulu had worn him out too.

"Hyperactive child with attention deficit

disorder," the doctor replied. "ADD, as we say in the business."

"Hey, I had that when I was a kid!" exclaimed Samir. "Year 5. *Hyperactive child* – they wrote it on my report!"

"Is it serious?" wondered Mrs Ben Azet, sounding like she guessed it was.

"Well, it's not something you catch, like chickenpox." Dr Andreas couldn't take his eyes off Lulu. "You do realize," he said, thinking out loud, "that this little girl was suffering from a terminal illness."

"That means there wasn't any cure for her," Samir translated.

"So she's supposed to be getting weaker," continued Dr Andreas. "She can't ... she's not meant to be able to jump about like that." He sounded like he was blaming her. Lulu was a kick in the teeth of medical science. "I need to examine her," he sighed, "but…"

But Lulu just kept bouncing.

And bouncing.

And bouncing…

"Don't touch her!" warned Samir. "You'll get a mega shock."

"I beg your pardon?"

"Lulu's gone electric," Mrs Ben Azet told him, rather like she might have said "She's started wetting the bed."

"What d'you mean, *electric*?"

"She does light signals at the window," Samir explained. "With a bulb."

"You mean a torch," the doctor corrected him.

"No, just a bulb. She holds it between her fingers."

Dr Andreas smiled stupidly. Samir tried to reassure him. "It's just a glow, OK…"

All of a sudden the doctor stood up. "Just a minute, my little pumpkin. Lulu, can you stop for a second?" He held out his arms to steady the little girl. "Ouch!" He gazed at his hands in disbelief.

"Told you," said Samir smugly.

"It's not her fault," said Mrs Ben Azet. "She doesn't realize what she's doing. It's like she's not with us any more."

Dr Andreas cleared his throat. "I need to talk to you, Mrs Ben Azet. Alone." He looked at Samir.

"OK, I get it."

Samir opened the door. Oddly, Lulu seemed to have got it too. Without saying a word, she bounced after him into the living room.

Samir was annoyed with his little sister. After all he'd done for her, he thought she was well out of order to disrespect him like this, and shut herself up in her world of pure energy. "It's looking bad, sis," he said. "You gotta make an effort, coz otherwise…" He didn't finish what he was saying, but went over to the bedroom door instead and glued his ear to it.

"Doctor's saying cut out phosphates and sugar … eggs, milk, cheese, cakes, Big B cola… No way! That's everything nice!"

Lulu had turned to face her brother. For a split second she looked like she was paying attention.

"He's saying you're a special case … he's never seen anybody like you before…"

Lulu started bouncing about again on her multi-coloured ball.

"Mum wants to know what deficit disorder means. She says we've all got deficit problems since Dad lost his job. Stop jumping! I can't hear!"

Samir pressed one ear harder against the thin

door and stuck his finger in the other. He heard his mum complaining, saying Lulu was bankrupting them, making the electricity meter go into over-drive. Dr Andreas promised Mrs Ben Azet that Lulu wouldn't cost her anything from now on. He'd got a solution to her problems. Samir had to strain to catch the next part. The doctor and his mother were talking in increasingly hushed tones, like people with something to hide.

"On the holy Koran of Mecca!" yelped Samir. "They're going to lock you up in a hospital. Mum's agreed to sign the papers. Lulu! She's going to sell you to the doctors so they can do experiments on you!"

He could hear everything clearly again now, because Lulu had stopped making her racket. When he turned round, she'd disappeared.

"Lulu?"

Samir rushed out of the room. The door to the flat was wide open. The ball was making its way downstairs. *Boing! Boing!*

"*Aargh, ma-aa-an!*"

Samir's first reaction was to run after her. But he didn't want Lulu getting sent to hospital. He'd leave it to the grown-ups to try and catch her. He went back into the living room. Through the window he watched Lulu crossing the estate in gigantic leaps, bouncing past astonished passers-by. It was like a scene from a kids' story.

Samir knew where she was heading.

And she didn't have far to go.

Lulu left her ball at the entrance to the quarry. She continued on her short legs, glancing disapprovingly around her. Following that horrible BIT Arena, Joke's home was a dump. There was all kinds of junk strewn about: broken trestles tables, mangled cables, mauled banners, baseball caps advertising Big B Stores, empty cans … even a half-eaten sandwich.

She knew the way. At the back of the main area was the tunnel leading to the monster's lair. Lulu let out a cry of amazement. Joke didn't look like a friendly genie in a fairy tale now. More like a mountain of translucent jelly, with bluish glints. His gigantic pot belly almost filled the cave where he'd camped out. The air smelt funny, like after a violent thunderstorm.

She craned her neck in vain. She couldn't even see the head of her best friend in all the world. Had Joke registered she was there? There was nothing to indicate he had.

"Have you seen what you're like? Have you got any idea?" she asked reproachfully. "And now I've got Fosfates. They want to take me away to hospital."

The outsize blob shuddered. Joke's flabby body emitted a continuous noise, a sort of buzzing sound. Lulu didn't like feeling molested by a giant mosquito.

"We've got to put you on a diet," she insisted.

Joke's buzzing got louder and louder, until it was noisier than Mrs Ben Azet's old freezer.

"I can't understand what you're saying. Are you asleep? You've eaten too much, so you're having a rest. Is that right, Joke?"

A shower of crackling sparks was her only answer.

"Are you waking up now?"

The monster's belly was shaken by spasms riding in enormous trembling waves. Suddenly, the air around Lulu seemed to rip apart. There was an explosion and the little girl was hurled backwards several metres.

"Joke? Joke?" she whimpered. "You're scaring me." She was wrapped in smoke. "I'm not feeling well." She'd have been hard pushed to describe what she was experiencing. Maybe it was that illness the doctor had been talking about. She felt horribly hyperactive, but she couldn't move any more. She was trembling. The energy was in her body, running through her nerves. The energy was eating her up.

The last thing she heard was a growling noise coming from Joke's belly. A long, long roll of thunder…

Samir had cracked under pressure. Faced with his mum's anger, and Dr Andreas's veiled threats, he'd ended up admitting he knew where Lulu had run away to. The doctor had called an ambulance, and the large white vehicle was now heading towards the quarry.

Samir prayed he hadn't made a terrible mistake. How could he explain that Lulu needed to be near a creature from a computer game, who used high-voltage electricity lines to satisfy his appetite? What would happen to her when she was in hospital, far away from Joke? On the other hand, he realized his little sister was in trouble. Phosphates – yeah, right. Lulu had flipped. Burnt a fuse. She doesn't need a doctor, he thought, staring at the man in a white shirt driving the ambulance. What she needs is an electrician.

Samir had made them promise to let him go into the quarry alone. He'd insisted he was the only person Lulu would listen to. But as he was getting out of the ambulance, he wasn't so sure.

Ten minutes. His mum had given him ten minutes.

It took him less than two to find Lulu.

His little sister was lying splayed on the ground, close to a giant paw. He looked up and swallowed a cry of amazement. Godzilla would seem small next to Joke. The monster was dozing, sleeping off his electric blowout. Samir remembered the bootees Aisha had made. They'd barely cover one toe now.

Anxiously he made his way over to Lulu. She was still breathing. But she needed to get out of there fast. He'd have to deal with Joke later. They couldn't let him guzzle any more. If he went on swelling up at this rate, he'd go pop.

Samir bent down to lift Lulu. "Ou-uu-ch!" The pain shot right up to his shoulder. Like he'd stuck two fingers in a socket. Lulu was charged up to max. There was no way he could touch her.

He thought back to the bootees. To the outfit they'd made for Joke from fireproof survival blankets. He knew where to find it. They'd rolled it up into a ball and stuffed it in a hollow in the chalky wall. He headed back down the underground tunnel and found the big foil sheet sewn by Aisha into a ghost costume.

"There we go ... that's it..." He spread the blanket on the ground, near his sister's inert body. "Sorry, Lulu." He put the toe of his trainer under her side. He nudged her and she rolled over by herself. She weighed next to nothing. Then he folded over the sections of foil, wrapping her up tightly. When he lifted her off the ground, she let out a tiny whimper.

Behind her, Joke replied with a long sad grunt.

Outside, the doctor and ambulance man rushed over to their young patient.

"Don't touch her! Don't touch her!" shouted Samir.

They stepped back, bewildered, while he laid his little sister down in the back of the ambulance. Just as he was clambering in, he noticed another van out of the corner of his eye, parked near one of the high-voltage pylons. Moreland Electricity had sent a team out to investigate the disturbances reported by the local residents. Samir wondered how long it would take them to locate the source of the leak.

In no time, Lulu became a star attraction at the hospital. Nurses and doctors came to get a shock just by touching her with their fingertips. All the tests showed she was still suffering from the same terrible genetic disorder that had confined her to her bed for most of her short life. What did this hyperactive crisis, this exhausting overflow of energy, actually mean? Nobody knew the answer. They tried putting her on a phosphates-free diet, they tried drugs, but it was no good. Lulu called out for milk, cheese, chocolate and biscuits.

And she kept on producing electricity.

After a while the little girl grew less hungry. She became less agitated. She stopped giving such strong electric shocks. Was she bored? It was raining outside, and she watched the downpour from the window of her little hospital room.

It was raining and the Force was deserting her.

And the Winner Is...

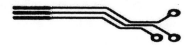

The manager of Moreland Town Big B Stores, Bernard Martin-Webber, was enjoying the view from his glass office. In a single glance he could take in nearly all the aisles, the swarming mass of customers and the checkout tills.

There was a festive mood at Big B Stores today. Banners, little flags strung across the aisles, giant posters, flashing lights and musical entertainment … it was Christmas in July. BMW didn't need to go down and join the crowd of consumers to feel the temperature rising. He knew all about it. Right now, everybody was chasing the same dream: to win one of the two trips to B Happy Land promised to the winners of Big B Stores' grand competition. First prize: a weekend for two. Second prize: a weekend for two.

It was some party. But Bernard Martin-Webber wasn't feeling his best. A few days earlier, while driving his flashy car, he'd hit a load of dustbins before crashing into a block of flats. He'd still got whiplash and a pain in his left elbow. But it wasn't the shunt that was making him feel uneasy. No. He was haunted by what had made him lose control of his vehicle in the first place. A horde of monsters from another world, feathery, creepy-crawly slimy creatures ... that bore an uncanny resemblance to the Evildoers from Golem.

BMW had been foolish enough to tell people what he'd seen. Then, realizing that they thought he was losing his mind, he'd decided he must have fallen asleep at the wheel. He desperately wanted to believe he had. But somehow he wasn't convinced. And he kept waking up with a start in the night.

A weekend at B Happy Land. "I could do with a break," he muttered. It might help him relax. But the trip wasn't for him, because the happy winners were...

BMW sniggered. Since the supermarket opened that morning, he'd been keeping an eye on those clever-clogs who were doing their shopping in dribs and drabs in order to pass through the check-out as many times as possible. They'd have bought a right sock first and then the left one if they could. Because today customers were given an envelope when they paid. Inside, everybody – or nearly everybody – found the same message:

Big B Stores thanks you
for your visit.
Better luck next time!

There were only five winning envelopes. Inside them it read:

CONGRATULATIONS!
You've been chosen to take part in our Big competition
to win a dream weekend at B Happy Land.
See you on the podium at 5 p.m.!

So far everything had gone to plan. Fortunately Big B Stores' loyal customers were creatures of habit.

Mrs Ben Azet had put in an appearance around midday, her trolley loaded with pasta shells and discounted wine. Mrs Ben Azet had been lucky. Mrs Ben Azet had been chosen.

"Aha!" BMW sounded relieved. "I thought she'd never show up." He'd just spotted Mrs Badach in the oils and condiments section.

Jacky put his hand to his earpiece to hear BMW's instructions more clearly.

"A well-built Fatima in a flowery dress … she always goes through checkout ten, Maya's till."

Jacky nodded in the direction of the glass office to show he'd understood.

Discreetly he slipped an envelope to Maya. More discreetly still, he whispered in the cashier's ear, "For Mrs Badach. No messing around, OK?" Then he positioned himself near the exit, microphone in his hand, ready to pounce. He reflected bitterly on what he was getting paid for the day. A lousy fee to rig a competition and ask housewives mindless questions. When all he dreamt of was prime-time TV and massive audience ratings.

Fatima just kept on stuffing her plastic bags.

Phew, finished at last. Maya held the envelope out. Glory be, she wasn't even going to open it! Jacky shot the cashier a meaningful glance as he approached Mrs Badach.

"Aren't you going to open it, Mrs Badach?" Maya asked placidly.

Emmay took the little card out of its envelope, but shook her head. "Majid he will read it me," she said.

Jacky appeared behind her. "So? Well?" he asked greedily.

Emmay shrugged. "Iz too difficult. Majid he will read it me."

Jacky leant over Mrs Badach's generous cleavage. "But hold on a second, it looks to me like … yes indeed, Mrs Badach, you've been chosen!"

"How you iz knowing my name? I iz not know-ing you!"

But Jacky wasn't listening. Jacky was getting carried away. He held the mike close and started shouting. "Cho-oo-sen! We've now got our fifth and final candidate in the competition for a dream weekend at B Happy Land! Ladies and gentlemen, please make your way over to our podium, where the grand competition will take place in just a few minutes' time. Which lucky winner will get to kiss Big B Teddy? Who will enjoy the terrifying experience of a ride in GruyèreLand? We're about to find out."

Mrs Badach was lagging behind the four other contestants. She was still complaining as she was pushed onto the podium. "But iz not possible! My hair iz so big mess!"

At last all five of them were lined up under the spotlights. Jacky could get started.

"What we've got for you today is a geography quiz in conjunction with our Big B world range. Mrs Biggins, if you passed our tea and coffee section, you must have spotted our special Costa Rican coffee offer: two packets for the price of one, until the end of the month. Mrs Biggins, can you name the capital of Costa Rica for us?"

Mrs Biggins bit her lip. Mrs Biggins fiddled with a wisp of her blonde hair, peered at the audience and let out a despairing sigh. Then she guessed. "Costa Rica City?"

Sadly it was San José. Mrs Biggins hadn't heard of San José. She was eliminated.

"But you're not going away empty-handed, Mrs Biggins. By way of a consolation prize, Big B Stores would like to offer you three pots of far— Ha ha! *Noisy* goo. Pick whatever colours take your fancy. See how fab the blue is – the kids go crazy for it. Step down from the podium now, Mrs Biggins."

Jacky tugged her by the arm to get her out of the way. Once he'd caught his breath, he turned to Emmay.

"Mrs Badach, you can't have missed our fantastic offer on Big B couscous: three bumper-size boxes for the price of two. Couscous as good as they make it back home. In fact, that's exactly my question. What's the capital of Algeria, Mrs Badach?"

Emmay was taken aback. What she really wanted to say was that her couscous was nothing like the revolting porridge sold at Big B Stores.

"Mrs Badach?" asked Jacky, hurrying her along.

"Well, iz easy, iz Algiers. Iz my city where I iz born! And my couscous it iz—"

"Is that your final answer?"

"Yes it iz, innit."

"Of course it is, Mrs Badach. Algiers! Give her a

round of applause! Wow! B Happy Land is getting closer!"

He turned to the third candidate. "Mrs O'Connor, I'm sure you find our famous Uzbekistani sausages as mouth-watering as the rest of us. Six for the price of four until the end of the month at our delicatessen counter. Ah! Uzbekistani smoked sausages! Mrs O'Connor, can you name the capital of Uzbekistan for me?"

A look of panic flashed in poor Mrs O'Connor's eyes. "Of where?"

"Come on now, Uzbekistan. I'll give you three more seconds. No whispering the answer, please!"

Nobody *was* whispering the answer.

"Tashkent, Mrs O'Connor! Tashkent! Oh, dearie me … step down, Mrs O'Connor. You'll also get three tubs of far— Ha ha! Noisy goo. Pick whatever colours you fancy. The kids go crazy for it."

Jacky wiped his brow and glanced at his prompt cards. "Mrs Ben Azet… D'you like pizzas, Mrs Ben Azet? Ah, I can see already the answer's yes. We've got a Neapolitan on special offer, half price in our frozen food section, so don't miss out. Pizza, Italy, gondolas, the Colosseum … it's enough to make you dream, isn't it? Mrs Ben Azet, can I have your undivided attention for a second? Can you tell me what's the capital of Italy?"

Mrs Ben Azet was like a block of marble on the podium. She showed no sign of having heard the question, just stared straight ahead.

"Mrs Ben Azet, the capital of Italy," he begged. "You know, the eternal city, it's got a name that sounds like a Caribbean drink … in the spirits aisle, Mrs Ben Azet. It's delicious with Big B cola or an exotic fruit juice…"

Mrs Ben Azet frowned and muttered something inaudible.

"Say that again, Mrs Ben Azet!"

"Rum?"

"Yes, you're absolutely right: rum, er, Rome! Rome! The capital of Italy! A round of applause, please!"

Jacky was beetroot. The sweat was pouring off him. But the end was in sight now. He just had to eliminate Mrs Goldberg. He wasn't worried about the fat woman in a shawl. Which was a mistake. Mrs Goldberg had spent thirty years as a geography teacher.

Calmly she listened to him singing the praises of noodles with baby vegetables from Malaya, available in freeze-dried packets from the world dishes aisle. When it was her turn to speak, she answered confidently.

"The capital of Malaya is Kuala Lumpur. But, technically speaking, we don't say Malaya any more, we say Malaysia."

"Ah? Really? Is ... er, er ... is that your final answer, Mrs Goldberg? Yes, I can see it is." Jacky tried desperately to catch the eye of BMW, who was watching the scene nervously, lost in the crowd.

"Well, we've narrowed it down to three contenders – three contenders for two trips of a lifetime to B Happy Land. Goodness me, the suspense is almost unbearable!" Frantically he consulted his prompt cards, looking for the questions he hadn't planned on asking.

"Mrs Herzog – whoops, sorry, I mean Mrs Goldberg, let's start with you this time. Naturally you're familiar with B Happy Land, the theme park for children and adults alike. The entrance fee's a bit hefty, but *what* a great place. Right, OK. Mrs Goldberg, can you give me the names of six of the six imaginary realms that make up B Happy Land?"

"Six out of six?" queried a surprised Mrs Goldberg.

"Six out of six," confirmed Jacky.

"But … that's not a geographical question."

"Oh yes it is! B Happy Land is a country, so it's geography, all right. B Happy Land, the country where Big B Teddy, My Little B Pony, Beautiful B and Fit B and Bumper Bird all live. Mrs Goldberg, please, you've got three seconds. No whispering at the back. Excellent, time's up! Take your pick. Ha ha! Kids go crazy for—"

"GruyèreLand!" called out Mrs Goldberg. "GruyèreLand!"

"It's too late. Step down now, please."

"But what about the others?" objected the retired teacher. "They haven't answered yet. You've got to ask them a question too!"

"There's no point. There are two dream trips to be won and there are two candidates left. Be reasonable, Mrs Goldberg. I'm sure you're disappointed but you'll get over it. Go on, pick the blue, the kids go crazy for it."

BMW had managed to drag the two happy winners into a function room away from the public, but not without a struggle. Not everybody was satisfied with the way the competition had been conducted. There'd been a few racist comments from the audience, along the lines of "If they'd wanted Arabs to win, why didn't they just say so?" But right now Bernard Martin-Webber had got his two prize winners, and the sense of mission accomplished filled him with relief.

Mrs Badach pushed away the glass of bubbly he was holding out to her.

"Well, my dear Mrs Badach, your Majid's going to be happy!"

Curiously, Fatima didn't exactly look over the moon. "Too lucky iz too lucky," she said meaningfully. BMW presumed that this was some kind of proverb from her country.

"Already Majid he iz winning komputer. Iz possible to give to Haziz?"

"Haziz?" he echoed, sounding alarmed. "Who's Haziz?"

"Iz other son. He iz come back. And now iz gone away again..."

"But he doesn't live with you, this Haziz of yours? This competition is only open to children who live in Moreland Town."

On the Ben Azet front, there was another nasty surprise. Mrs Ben Azet was already picturing herself at B Happy Land with her husband.

"It's for children!" said BMW, starting to lose his temper. "You're too old, Mrs Ben Azet, d'you understand? Too old!"

There was no time to lose. The trip to B Happy Land was scheduled for the following weekend. BMW wrapped things up briskly. At the end of the little prize-giving ceremony, the two winners held in their hands a travel itinerary, a daily programme, the official guide to B Happy Land, a forty-eight-hour pass and some meal vouchers.

Emmay was impressed by how efficient this B Corp outfit was. The name Majid Badach had already been printed on all the documents.

"I knew we were friends, but I didn't realize it went this far," said Sebastian.

"Nobody else to ask," Samir answered matter-of-factly.

"You should see your face! Nobody'd think you'd just got lucky."

Samir had dragged Sebastian into his little sister's bedroom without knowing why. He was sitting on Lulu's bed, kneading an old pair of pyjamas with pink rabbits all over them. Their familiar smell made him feel better. But it brought back memories too.

"Actually," pointed out Sebastian, "your mum was the lucky one."

"Yeah right, lucky... My mum didn't know what it meant till yesterday. She keeps going on about how they're gonna call up and say it's a mistake."

"I'll tell you who's on a winning streak, and that's Majid," said Sebastian.

"D'you think it'll work out for Aisha?"

Samir hadn't wasted any time in choosing. His partner for the weekend would be Sebastian. Majid hadn't taken much longer. But Aisha's parents were as strict as Sebastian's were cool. In fact, Mrs Badach was supposed to be round at her neighbours' across the landing right now, with a plate of gazelle horns.

Majid had folded and refolded his T-shirts and jeans, rolled his socks into balls and read the large piece of paper detailing their daily programme ten times over. Emmay had been round at Aisha's for more than an hour now. When she finally came back, there was a glimmer of something in her eye he'd rarely seen: anger.

"Iz not possible people like that!"

For a moment, Majid thought she'd failed. But he knew he could count on his mum. She'd have spent the whole night negotiating for him if she'd had to.

"Poor littel girl, iz like slave." Emmay grumbled on in this fashion for a minute or two before announcing the good news. Aisha *would* be going to B Happy Land after all. "I say to mummy, 'Iz boring without Majid. Maybe I drop by to looking after ze littel childrin.' Iz not possible people like that!"

"They got you!"

Emmay shrugged and sighed. "Iz true, Majid. Iz boring for me. You iz never away from home. All the others, they iz gone. And now iz you."

Majid threw his arms around his mum's neck. "But it's only for two days, Emmay! Two days!"

"Childrin, we know when they iz going, but we not know when they iz coming back."

Strangely, her words upset Majid.

On Friday evening, just before they had to leave, the three boys met up round at the Badachs'. They had a couple of things on their minds. Or rather, a couple of beings. Who couldn't have been more different, but who were linked in a mysterious fashion. One of them was in a dark cave. The other was in a sinister hospital. Who was going to keep an eye on Joke? Who would visit Lulu? They were only going away for two days. But two days that meant being hundreds of miles away from the Moreland Estate. Two days could be a very long time.

Majid had no trouble persuading his friends: only one person in the world would understand how worried they were.

Late Friday evening, Hugh picked up the following email:

Dear Cali,

We're off. We're all going on the dream weekend to B Happy Land. We means me and Aisha and Samir and Sebastian. We're going to have a heavy time. Except we're worried about Joke. Samir says he's seen him and he's big now. Even bigger than before. We're scared of him leaving the quarry by himself, because then he'd look like a real baddie. Like Godzilla – have you seen the film? Samir says we've got to put him on a diet. Could you ask Moreland Electricity to turn down the volume, you get me, so the current's not so strong? Or else we'll have to put chains on him like in *King Kong* at the end, but that'd be a shame. Specially for Lulu. The thing is, Samir's worried about Lulu too. She's going to be all on her own for two days. Fancy paying her a visit in hospital? She LIKES toffees, don't say I didn't tell you. B Happy Land isn't even in this country. I can't believe we're catching a plane! Six o'clock this evening!

Your friend Magic Majid!

PS dont wory abowt the speleng Seb woz
corictin me ova my showlda. Im stil normul.

Hugh frowned. B Happy Land? What on earth was
going on? He glanced at his rows of encyclopedias
and dictionaries. No good looking there.

It was early. He went to make a cup of coffee
to clear his thoughts. When he came back and sat
down in front of his computer, he typed the phrase
B Happy Land into his Internet search engine.

He had no problem finding the site. A brightly
coloured map gave the theme park's precise location.

In Switzerland.

Not far from Gruyères.

"Gruyères," he whispered. "B Corp... The
children!"

His hand reached for the phone. No. No point.
They'd already left.

The people carrier was speeding along the motorway. Aisha clutched her sports bag, her eyes fixed
on the road. The boys were cracking jokes. They
were buzzing with excitement. None of them had

ever been in a plane before. None of them had ever travelled abroad.

"Sir, sir, when'll we be there?" asked Samir.

"Sir, sir, we're not gonna miss the plane?" Majid worried.

Their driver glanced in his rear-view mirror. "Hey, kids! You're not going to call me sir for the whole trip, are you?"

"What's your name, sir?"

"Eddie."

Natasha Does Some Damage

Nadia dozed off briefly on Friday evening, only to wake up with a thick head. Albert had snored non-stop during their catnap. There was a storm coming. A bluebottle had got in. And sleeping three centimetres below the ceiling felt like lying in your own coffin.

"Right, that's it." She half sat up, and a raging migraine kicked in. A waft of fresh air reached her. "Albert. Albert?"

He was sitting in the doorway, the laptop balanced on his knees. "Present and correct." He was checking out a website dedicated to B Corp. The site's authors listed all the rumours created by Albert.

But, most important of all, they demonstrated that Golem did contain subliminal imaging and concluded: *The Trading Standards Authority is considering banning the sale of farting goo, which is thought to contain hallucinogenic substances.*

"Tonight's the last night I'm going to spend in this lousy camper van," he complained.

"Tonight's the last night I'm going to spend with *you*." Right now, Nadia loathed Albert.

"I'd be surprised," he answered. "Didn't I tell you I'm going to marry you?"

She couldn't help laughing. She climbed down off her perch and snuggled up next to him. "It's exhausting living with you," she whispered in his ear.

"Tell me about it! But at least you can take a break. I can't even do that."

Nadia rubbed her pounding head against his shoulder. She did love him, after all.

"Hey up, here comes Thingy," said Albert, spotting Hugh walking towards them.

Nadia could tell straight away that something was wrong. "Is it the dwagon?" she asked.

Hugh was taken aback. "No, the children,

Majid, B Corp..." he stammered.

"What's he on about?" whispered Albert. But he'd already stood up.

"The kids won a competition at Big B Stores," explained Hugh. "From what I've heard, it was rigged. They won a trip to B Happy Land. They've already left."

"They're closing in," Albert muttered.

"Surely they wouldn't do anything to harm the childwen!" objected Nadia.

Albert scowled. He knew B Corp. "I'm going to get them back," he announced.

Nadia clasped her hands and held them to her heart. She didn't say "My hero!" but it was what she meant.

"I'm going too," declared Hugh.

Albert frowned. Two heroes were one too many.

"They don't know me at B Corp," argued Hugh. "I'll be useful to you when we get there."

Albert didn't need convincing about Nadia. He couldn't bear to be separated from her now.

"If you're taking your girlfriend, then so am I," Hugh decided.

Nadia and Albert looked at each other, astonished. Hugh blushed.

"I mean, I'm taking my computer."

Mrs Mullins was delighted to hear her son was heading off on a weekend break with two friends, even if the trip was slightly disappointing from a cultural point of view.

"The country of Beautiful B and Big B Teddy," she said wonderingly, flicking through the brochure.

"And Bumper Bird," added Hugh.

As a psychologist, Mrs Mullins knew you shouldn't question your children too much about their friends. She needed a roundabout way of satisfying her curiosity. "Anybody I know?"

"Yes, Nadia Martin…"

Mrs Mullins clasped the brochure to her chest. Nadia, the charming science teacher! "I knew it!"

Hugh gave his mother a glazed look. Knew what? "She's bringing her boyfriend." He laughed nervously.

"Goodness!" exclaimed Mrs Mullins. Hugh was going away with a couple. It was rather odd. "How are you getting there?" she asked unsteadily.

"In a camper van."

"In..." It was very odd indeed. "Is that your luggage?" she asked, pointing to a large cardboard box.

"Yeah, I'm taking my computer. So I won't feel stupid." Hugh could tell from the way his mother was gazing at him that she hadn't followed his logic. "You know, I mean, Albert's got Nadia, and I'll have..." He was just about to mention Natasha when he remembered his mother wasn't up to speed on everything. In fact, he remembered she wasn't up to speed on anything.

"You'll have your computer," sighed a disheartened Mrs Mullins.

Hugh had a thought just before he set off. *What about the dragon?*

"Mum, can I leave Bubble with you?"

As far as Mrs Mullins was concerned, Bubble was a Sumatran dragon, a tiny exotic animal in danger of becoming extinct. Looking after him was a major responsibility. "You'll have to tell me exactly what he eats."

"Nothing."

"Nothing?"

"Yes, I know it doesn't sound much," said Hugh, tying himself up in knots. "But Sumatran dragons are a type of miniature boa constrictor. They eat a huge amount in one meal, and then starve themselves for a month."

"Really? Well, just a bit of water, then?"

"Absolutely not! Sumatran dragons are scaled-down versions of dromedaries. They store water in a subcutaneous lump by their tail. They're most unusual."

"And when it needs to spend a penny, I—"

"You don't do anything at all. Sumatran dragons eat their own excrement. Scientists have compared them to self-cleaning ovens. In miniature, of course."

"Well, as animals go, they're certainly…"

"Most unusual."

With Bubble taken care of, Hugh wanted to get back to Albert and Nadia. But Mrs Mullins clung to her son's arm. "Is everything all right, Hugh?"

"Yes, Mum."

"You're not hiding anything from me?"

"Of course not." He gave her a farewell peck on the cheek. As he was walking out of the door, he turned round. "I just wanted to say, Mum, thanks for making me so happy as a kid, even with Dad dying and all that."

And then he was gone.

"Guess who's coming to dinner?" Albert said to Nadia. "Thingy with his girlfriend. She looks like she weighs a ton."

"Go and give him a hand instead of talking wubbish."

Hugh was working his way down the row of vehicles, struggling under the weight of his BIT computer. Inside the camper van, he found Nadia and Albert had bagged the double bed. There were just the two window seats left, which converted into single beds. He put the computer down on one of them. Albert could see it wouldn't be long before Thingy asked for a blanket to tuck his monitor in. But he thought better of making a joke about it. He felt uneasy about Hugh's relationship with the virtual world. For all he knew, Golem's ally might turn into a very powerful man one of these days.

Most of Hugh's driving experience involved a

computer game version of the Monaco Grand Prix, so Albert took the wheel. Nadia, meanwhile, tried to get Hugh to talk. In a friendly gesture, she patted the electric blue monitor.

"Natatha's inside, is she?"

Hugh smiled.

"How does she get out?"

He looked defiant. "I make her come out." Nobody knew his secret. He was now the Master Golem.

Nadia sidled up to him, her eyes sparkling inquisitively. "Thugh, don't you want to tell me—"

"No." The young English teacher was hunched up on the window seat.

"If something happened to you, we wouldn't be able to get Natatha out again. You type *Alias* into the computer, and then?"

"You're wasting your time."

Nadia lost her temper. "And you're being stupid! What's happening to us is dangewous. Don't you wealize that? The virtual's starting to take over! B Corp's behind all of this and they'll stop at nothing!"

Hugh shook his head stubbornly.

"Yes, I'm telling you!" Nadia punched his shoulder. What a mess she was in – caught between a macho man and an overgrown teenager.

Over supper, which they ate in a motorway services car park, Albert pretended to feed the computer. "One spoonful for Daddy, one for Mummy and—"

"Natasha isn't virtual," Hugh interrupted. "She could blow your face up with her eraser-laser."

"Meaning?"

"Look, instead of winding each other up," Nadia interrupted, "why don't you think about how you're going to get the kids back?"

"Albert's going to parachute into B Happy Land and take Big B Teddy hostage," sniggered Hugh.

Albert glanced at Nadia. "He's a real pain in the neck."

At dawn the camper van crossed the Swiss border. Nadia had taken over from Albert at the wheel, and she pulled into a lay-by about fifteen miles from the theme park. The two drivers needed to get some sleep, and climbed wearily up into the double bed.

Hugh waited until he could hear regular breathing. Then he left his bed and crept over to his computer. He felt dreadfully lonely, far away from his mother.

"Natasha," he whispered.

He disconnected the little fridge and plugged in his computer. He didn't know what he was going to do yet. As soon as the screen started flashing, the five-pointed star appeared with its message:

I am that which is known by another name.

Hugh typed **Alias**.

Enter your name.

He didn't even think about it, just typed the word that would deliver his princess: **Calimero**.

The computer started purring, projecting the image of Natasha into the air, her eraser-laser resting on her hip, and her shorts and strappy top hugging her curvy figure. Then the beam was sucked back in. The process of materialization got faster and more accurate every time. But Natasha's first gesture always had the grace of a dreamer slowly waking up. In the darkness of the camper van, a blue-white halo outlined her body. Hugh watched, open-mouthed. What had he done? What was he going to do?

"Natasha?" he whispered.

She'd seen him. This time he didn't need to do anything, because she was the one who held out a hand to him. She stroked the air around the young teacher, tracing the shape of his cheek, his shoulder. Then she placed a finger on his lips. Hugh could feel it now. Her finger pressed down on his mouth, inviting silence. But it was cold and it crackled.

"Hugh," she said. Her voice came out low-pitched, but still rather metallic. He trembled. "You are … human." She pronounced the word human like somebody who'd just discovered it, trying it out for the first time. She let her hand wander over his face, pushing her fingertips into his cheeks and stroking his forehead.

"Human," she whispered.

"I love you," he said.

"I love you," she echoed back.

"My love."

"My love."

He smiled. She smiled. A man and a woman. Almost.

The spell was broken by a ghastly shriek. In the double bed overhead, Nadia had woken up and seen a shape radiating blue light.

Peowww! The eraser-laser fired its beam.

"Nadia, get down!" shouted Hugh.

Peowww! Peowww!

"Reload," echoed Natasha's hollow voice.

"No, stop!" Hugh begged. "They're allies. Stop!"

Peowww! Peowww! A deluge of blue-white fire crashed around the camper van. Nadia and Albert huddled against the wall. Albert cried out as the laser beam hit him on the arm while he was trying to protect Nadia. The burning sensation was terrible and his flesh started peeling apart.

"Water!" shouted Hugh. "Throw water on her!"

Peowww! Peowww! Reload.

Hugh crawled towards a bottle of mineral water. But Natasha destroyed it before he could get there. There was only one thing to do.

He stood up, holding out his arms. "Go on, kill me."

Peowww! The beam missed him. Natasha lowered her weapon. "You are … human."

"Yes. And those other two are human as well. They've only got one life, like me. You've got to understand—"

"I'm dying here," interrupted a terrified Albert. The wound in his arm was opening up, as if an invisible scalpel was continuing the damage inflicted by the eraser-laser.

"Thugh, it's awful!" sobbed Nadia. She forgot how frightened she was of the girl-golem. All she knew was that Albert was being sliced in half.

"Can't you see?" shouted Hugh. "Can't you see what you've done?"

"Do I get a bonus?" Natasha asked.

Albert was gasping with pain. Nadia was sobbing.

"Do something, just do something," pleaded Hugh.

Natasha climbed the steps and bent over Albert, who was writhing on the bed. There were ten little flasks hanging off her belt. She unhooked one and tipped it over the wound. What came out was a splash of light. In a few seconds, the wound closed and all trace of the burn disappeared.

"It's gone!" shouted Nadia, still sobbing. "She's cured him!"

"I won those first-aid kits in the game," Hugh remembered.

Albert propped himself up on one elbow, his features still twisted from the horror he'd been through. "We've got to destroy her," he whispered to Hugh, thinking Natasha couldn't understand.

He was answered by an ominous-sounding *click-clack*. Natasha was reloading her eraser-laser.

"No water," she said metallically.

"She can help us," pleaded Hugh. "She's a ... friend." He didn't sound very sure. In the middle of the camper-van-cum-battlefield, he was having second thoughts.

Natasha was still perched on the ladder. She was looking at Nadia and Albert, who were hugging each other.

"Human," she said, in the voice of somebody waking from a dream.

A Matter of Days

Mrs Mullins couldn't explain why Hugh leaving made her feel so sad. Early the next morning she decided to pull herself together by doing a spot of tidying. I'll start with Hugh's study, she thought. As a psychologist, she knew that parents shouldn't pry into their children's secrets. So she tried not to look at anything too closely. The letter lying on his desk and the printout were nothing to do with her. She edged nearer and saw that the printout was an email. Not that it mattered what it said, because she wasn't interested.

We're off. We're all going on the dream weekend to B Happy Land.

The words B *Happy Land* made Mrs Mullins shudder. That was where Hugh was going. She grabbed the email and read every word.

> We means me and Aisha and Samir and Sebastian.

Hugh's students were going to B Happy Land too. What a strange coincidence.

Majid – the email was from him – was talking nonsense about one of their friends whose nick-name seemed to be Joke. Mrs Mullins read this section absent-mindedly, but frowned when Majid mentioned Lulu in hospital. She knew about Samir's little sister, who was terminally ill with a genetic disorder. She also knew that Mr and Mrs Ben Azet weren't very responsible parents, and she resolved to pay Lulu a visit that afternoon. She'd take her some toffees. But no sooner had she decided this than her gaze fell on Bubble's crate. Hugh wasn't very concerned about the tiny animal.

"That box is titchy!" she declared. It was cruel to leave the poor Sumatran dragon in a prison with just a few holes punched in it. "What if he's thirsty after all?" she wondered aloud.

She put a saucer of water on Hugh's desk and opened the box a crack. Bubble lifted his head. Mrs Mullins gave a cry of surprise. The dragon was running very low on electricity. He was slowly turning back into a hologram and the light seemed to pass straight through him. Recognizing the boss with the broom, the one who'd scored a victory by shutting him in the microwave, he huddled fearfully in a corner of the crate.

"Ickle-lickle! Ickle-lickle!" cooed Mrs Mullins, trying to reassure him. She offered him the saucer.

Water! She wanted to destroy him. Bubble pretended to be dead, muzzle between his paws, eyes closed.

"Ickle-lickle! Ickle…"

There was a soppy side to Mrs Mullins. Unwisely she stroked the dragon's neck and felt an unpleasant tingling sensation. She remembered Hugh's warning. The little animal was poisonous. She panicked and ran into the kitchen, where she dunked her hand in a bowl of icy water.

Bubble opened an eye. He needed his electricity hit, and he knew where the recharging terminal was.

Just one problem: the boss. She switched levels so quickly it was basically cheating. He glanced anxiously at the door and put his front paws on the edge of the crate, ready to leap.

Too late. She was back!

"Ickle-lickle!" chirruped Mrs Mullins. "You've moved again. You're a sly one, that's for sure."

Bubble decided to go for it. He opened his mouth and spat a feeble flame.

Mrs Mullins took a step back. "What's going on?"

Bubble jumped out of the crate and trotted over to the chest of drawers, where his lifeline was: an electric socket. He jammed in his tail. Boy, did that feel good! The bonus to beat all bonuses.

While he powered up, Bubble had disconnected. He was in down-time mode. Mrs Mullins, who was now lying flat on the floor, had an unrestricted view of an extraordinary spectacle: a Sumatran dragon recharging his batteries. Hugh wasn't there this time to pretend that Bubble was closely related to the electric eel. This animal wasn't unusual. It was unreal.

A shiver ran down her spine. She'd just made

a strange connection. What was it Majid had said in his email? She picked up the piece of paper again.

> Except we're worried about Joke... Could you ask Moreland Electricity to turn down the volume, you get me, so the current's not so strong?

Mrs Mullins hadn't yet imagined the unimaginable, but she wasn't far off.

After lunch, she made sure Hugh's study door was shut, put on a yellow cagoule and set off for the hospital. She stopped off at a sweet shop to buy some gooey toffees. Back outside, she'd barely taken three steps before she was drenched.

It was no weather for a dragon to be out in.

At reception they were pleased that the little Ben Azet girl finally had a visitor.

"Are you his mother?" asked the nurse.

From which Mrs Mullins deduced that Mrs Ben Azet hadn't bothered to come and see her own child. "I'm a friend," she said. "How's Lulu doing?"

"That's the problem. We've been trying to get

hold of her parents since yesterday. They're never home."

Mrs Mullins looked at the pretty bag of toffees tied up with a ribbon. "But what about her?" she asked.

The nurse looked away. "It's a matter of days…"

Lulu's energy had gone again. She was dying.

"Can I see her?"

The nurse broke into a broad smile. "Of course! She doesn't get many visitors."

Since the disease had re-established itself, Lulu was no longer an interesting case. She was being left to die in peace and quiet.

Mrs Mullins only knew the little girl from what Hugh had told her. She felt a pang of anguish when she saw Lulu looking frail and washed out under a white sheet. A drip was maintaining the fluid levels in her tiny body.

"Is she suffering?" she asked.

"No, no," answered the nurse, before making a quick escape.

Abandoned. That was the word that came into Mrs Mullins's mind. An abandoned child. Like a neglected patch of garden. Or a dog on the side of the road. She put the toffees on the bedside table and sat by the bed. She clasped her hands in her lap, closed her eyes and thought of the husband she'd looked after throughout his long illness. This little girl was going to die, and there'd be nobody watching lovingly over her. Mrs Mullins had a feeling it wasn't just chance that had brought her to Lulu. She opened her eyes and gently ran her hand through the little girl's curls. Was it possible? She felt that tingling sensation in her fingertips again. Lulu … Bubble…

Lulu spoke. "Joke…"

Mrs Mullins leant over her. "What did you say, dear?"

"Mummy," whispered Lulu, "you've got to save Joke." She seemed far away in a dream. "Joke's all woozy. That's why I haven't got the Force any more, Mummy."

"You'll feel better soon," Mrs Mullins lied. "That's what the doctors said."

"The doctors don't understand," Lulu rasped. "Somebody's got to go and feed Joke."

Mrs Mullins wondered whether the little girl had a hamster or goldfish at home she was worrying about. But this explanation didn't entirely satisfy her. Majid's email had also mentioned a Joke.

"Is he in your bedroom?" she asked, not sure if Lulu could hear her.

The little girl gave a feeble smile, without opening her eyes. "No, Mummy, he's in the quarry."

Mrs Mullins felt the answer was within reach. But like in a fairground maze, she kept coming up against one glass wall, then another.

"You've got to do it quickly, Mummy," whispered the little girl.

"It's a matter of days," the nurse had said.

Mrs Mullins stood up. Do *what* quickly?

"Give me a kiss, Mummy," demanded Lulu. She kept her eyes shut, so she could pretend her mum had come to see her. Mrs Mullins brushed her cheek with her lips and got a tiny shock.

Instead of going directly home, Mrs Mullins made a detour via the old abandoned quarry. It was such a strange place she was tempted to get out of her car and take a closer look. But the storm kicked back in. A roll of thunder. Then, like an echo, she thought she heard a kind of wailing: it gave her goose pimples. She vowed to come back another time, when the rain had stopped, and get to the bottom of the mystery behind that mischievous name: Joke.

If she'd made it as far as the main dugout, Mrs Mullins would have seen a sorry sight. There'd been so much rain recently, it had seeped in through the cracks in the roof. The remains of the BIT Arena were floating in a lake at the entrance to the tunnels.

Joke hadn't been able to leave his den for several days now. Water was pouring in, spreading right, left and centre, stopping him from binge-eating at the Moreland Electricity pylon.

It was starving him.

When he got near the little lake, Joke could see his reflection. Each day he looked shorter. Each day he looked thinner.

And it wasn't just electricity he was hungry for. Something else was missing too. Perched on a rock at the water's edge he held out his arms and wailed heartbreakingly, "Friend … friend…"

Back in the flat, Bubble was psyching himself up for the return of the enemy. Charged to max and on sizzling form, he trotted between the furniture with the energy of a lizard dashing between rocks. From time to time, just for kicks, he spat his miniature flame and surveyed the hole burnt in the carpet with satisfaction. It did have its good points, this game.

"Such a nuisance, this thingy!" exclaimed Mrs Mullins when she spotted him. She ran to get the broom. Bubble rose up proudly on his hind legs, thinking he'd scared her off.

"Pssst! Go on, shove off!"

Uh-oh! The mega-powerful weapon! Bubble flattened himself on the carpet as a sign of surrender and started purring like a defenceless kitten.

"What a pest," muttered Mrs Mullins. She poked the broom handle in the beastie's side a few times, and the purring was interspersed with whining. "I'll put you back in your box," she decided.

Prison? Uh-oh! Bubble'd had it up to here with that place. He flattened himself a tiny bit more and endured the broom handle prodding without budging an inch. Purr, purr, whine, whine.

Mrs Mullins gave up on the idea of getting him back inside the crate. She'd just caught sight of Majid's email again. She reread it, trembling.

> Except we're worried about Joke. Samir says he's seen him and he's big now. Even bigger than before. We're scared of him leaving the quarry by himself…

An extraordinary world was opening up before Mrs Mullins, but her mind refused to make the leap.

The sound of trotting paws made her look down. Bubble had edged right up to her. He was lying at her feet, staring up imploringly. This was getting embarrassing. Mrs Mullins had never persecuted another living being before. But *was* this a living being?

The sound of the phone ringing distracted her.

"Hugh!"

Unfortunately it was the features editor of *Psychology: Keys to the Mind*, who was expecting an article about the dangers computer games pose to children.

"What dangers?" asked Mrs Mullins.

The features editor was taken aback. "You know perfectly well. The risk of confusing the real with the virtual—"

Mrs Mullins cut her short. "There's no risk."

Bubble had adopted a sit-up-and-beg position in front of her.

"I think you need to qualify what you're saying. The games are sometimes so realistic, children run the risk of—"

Click. Mrs Mullins hung up. She bent down and scratched the carpet. "Ickle-lickle! Ickle-lickle!"

The tiny dragon slumped back down on all fours and came even closer. He was so tame! She set off towards the kitchen and Bubble followed. Her little companion made her realize how lonely she really felt.

When night began to fall, she opened her bedroom door. A delighted Bubble was convinced he'd discovered the last set of graphics for the game. Without saying a word, Mrs Mullins pushed aside the armchair covering a socket that was at just the right height for a miniature dragon. Whatever floats your boat, she thought.

At the hospital, the nurse who'd come to tuck Lulu in for the night noticed that the little girl wasn't electric at all any more. Everything was back to normal. Joke and Lulu were disconnected.

Death was fast becoming a reality.

In the Claws of B Corp

Samir, Majid, Sebastian and Aisha landed at Lausanne late on Friday night. But their journey wasn't over. The next morning B Happy Land laid on a helicopter for the last thirty-five miles. Jason, the pilot, had a strong American drawl.

"Hey, kiddiewinks, hold on tight!"

Aisha screamed. The helicopter looked like it was heading straight for a rocky peak. It swerved at the last moment.

Jason grinned. "The last time I did that, the door was open. Let's hope he landed in snow, or he'd have done himself some serious damage. Ha ha!"

"Jason likes a good joke," said Eddie, without smiling.

"Check that out! Kinda beautiful, hey?" exclaimed Jason.

The children looked where he was pointing and saw the six imaginary realms that made up B Happy Land. Shiny domes, turrets, giant statues, magic fairground rides and miniature lakes nestling in a green landscape. At nine thirty in the morning the lakes still looked calm. But a queue over a hundred metres long had already formed in front of the main entrance.

Aisha, Samir, Majid and Sebastian were no ordinary visitors. They didn't have to jostle with the crowds or hang around. Their passes fast-tracked them to the VIP check-in. B Happy Land was theirs for two days. At the B Gifted shop they were given their Life is Big B T-shirts.

Majid wanted to explore ComputerLand, Samir was into the idea of BankLand, Sebastian thought FutureLand would be his kind of place, and Aisha was dreaming of Beautiful B's palace, whose towers rose up above FunLand.

"My dad said we should stay together," she said.

"What about GruyèreLand?" suggested Eddie. "You can go tobogganing in the giant Gruyère. And afterwards you can visit the workshop where they make rounds of cheese that weigh as much as one of you!" He glanced at his watch. He'd got two hours to kill. Two hours before he had to take the children to FutureLand. He must keep them busy somehow.

The cheese-making workshop didn't get many votes. "Look!" he said. "There's Big B Teddy and Bumper Bird! D'you want to shake their paws? I know – why don't I take a photo?"

The three boys from Moreland Town gave the squidgy furry animals heading their way a look of disgust.

"Die, more like," said Majid.

"Isn't there anything scary?" asked Samir.

"Sure," Eddie reassured him. "But you'd better take it easy to start with. Here, let's catch this train. Climb on." He would never have admitted it, but he hated the Rails of Death and the House of Horror. Even as a kid he used to scream when he was taken on rides at the fair.

To see all the different attractions, they went round the park in a mini red and yellow carriage at the grand speed of eight miles an hour. They saw BankLand with its roulette wheel that spun you round while you were strapped inside a giant marble. ConsumerLand with its outsize Big B Stores where electric trolleys carried shoppers between the aisles. FunLand with its giant human body where you entered via the mouth and came out through the intestines to rude sound effects.

When they reached the Big B terminus, Eddie looked at his watch. They'd still got over an hour to kill.

Samir nudged him. "OK, what's a heavy thing to do next?"

"The farting goo parade's about to start."

But the boys had spotted the entrance to the House of Horror. Eddie would happily have waited for the kids at the exit. There was no chance of them disappearing: they'd be strapped into their seats. But he couldn't risk disobeying orders.

The children stamped their feet with excitement as the infernal caterpillar train swooshed into the darkness. One brush with the spiders' webs and their laughter died. It was as if each of them had an appointment with their own ghost. In a sinister ballroom where Death led the dance, Aisha saw small puffs of blue smoke, like the ones she'd noticed wafting on her landing. Turning the bend, Samir and Sebastian found themselves eye to eye with a fluorescent ghost. For a split second they thought they were reliving their first encounter with the golem in the basements of Hummingbird Tower. The House of Horror caterpillar was travelling so fast it was going back in time.

Majid looked round. A man had hoisted himself up just behind him, a pale killer with red eyes. It was Klaus, the fake delivery man who worked for B Corp.

"Emmay!" he yelped.

But his assailant was just a skeleton hanging from the end of a rope.

Eddie was welded to his seat, determined to open only one eye. But he was forced to open the other one too. The Evildoers were back! Just like in Moreland Town, when they'd showed up in the glare of his headlights. A furious mass of fur and claws. He lashed out to try and get rid of them, but it was no good. You can't hurt holograms.

When they emerged from the House of Horror, everybody burst out laughing in a forced kind of way.

"Shall we check out the rides at the fairground, kiddos?" suggested Eddie.

"How about the Shuttle in Distress?" asked Samir, ogling a space capsule that was spinning fifty metres above the ground.

"No, no. I've got a better ride. With giraffes and dromedaries."

Eddie's face was the colour of an overripe kiwi fruit. Nobody wanted to contradict him.

At twenty-five past eleven, Eddie gathered his young posse together. "Now things start getting serious," he said, pointing at the sparkling dome that towered over FutureLand, the most state-of-the-art realm in the theme park. "The B Max! Look at it, just look at it!"

What the children saw was the endless queue in front of the silver doors.

"Look, can you see how disappointed they are? Closed! The B Max is closed! And d'you know why?"

"Go on, tell us," grumbled Samir.

"Because it's all yours! Just for you, Samir. And you, Majid."

"Hey! What about us?" chorused Sebastian and Aisha.

Eddie gestured mysteriously. "Your turn will come ... later. We've got a surprise for them ... a surprise for two people. Majid and Samir are our two big winners, aren't they? Respect to the winners!"

"But my dad said—" Aisha started.

Eddie cut her off. "You won't be on your own. Sebastian'll be with you. I'm sure you must both be hungry. I'll take you to the Mega B Café."

Majid felt his own stomach rumbling, but he didn't dare say anything. He was too excited about the surprise for two people.

The vast B Max auditorium was deserted. Eighty empty seats facing a giant screen.

Deserted? Not quite. There was somebody up in the projection room. And it wasn't the projectionist.

The man watching the two Big B Stores prize winners walk in was called Orwell. For those in the know, he was the butler-cum-personal-assistant to Mr William, the head of B Corp. But not many people were in the know.

So here they are, thought Orwell. Majid Badach and Samir Ben Azet. Two kids, two scrawny scumbags from the suburbs. Two grains of sand that had jammed the smooth workings of B Corp. Orwell couldn't believe how young they were. But at the same time, he remembered they were Sven's killers, the kids who'd driven Klaus to the end of the line, who'd hijacked the precious New Generation BIT computer, who'd let a horde of electronic demons loose – how had they managed it? – on an entire estate and its surroundings. Two grains of sand that needed sweeping up.

But not just yet.

"Make yourselves comfortable, boys," Eddie told them. "There. And there. This is going to be an unforgettable experience." He couldn't help laughing. "Unforgettable," he repeated.

"What you doing?" Majid was alarmed. "Don't tie me up!"

"Shh! Shh!" hissed Eddie. "The B Max, kids. The most ultra-modern attraction on the planet! I can plug you directly into it, are you following me?"

"But I'm not sick!" complained Samir. Eddie had wrapped a thick band around his arm. He recognized it: the doctor put the same thing around Lulu's arm when he took her blood pressure.

"You're going on a journey to the stars," Eddie explained. "Top astronauts don't get better kit than this."

Majid and Samir had wires tied around their chests now. Eddie attached something to the fingers on their right hands.

"What *is* this, the electric chair?" Samir was getting annoyed.

"Just electrodes, my friend, that's all."

"But ... electrodes are ... electric!"

"Open your eyes. We're about to take off."

The B Max auditorium went dark. The film started. And, just like that, the two viewers forgot everything else as they dived into the extraordinary world of a space station. BIT Galactic was taking them on a gripping voyage.

It was beautiful and peaceful to start with. The BIT *Starship* was a gigantic vessel that travelled from star to star. For a few minutes, Majid and Samir were lulled into thinking they were space pioneers, setting off to explore the galaxy. But then they entered a belt of asteroids and flew into a violent magnetic storm.

The spaceship was caught up in terrifying turbulence. The two passengers clutched the arms of their chairs. But nothing could bring them back to earth now. They were being rocked in their seats, swayed with the BIT *Starship*, each hail of meteorites shaking them to the bone. When the vessel dived into a canyon with steep sides several miles high, they thought they were done for. When a stray rock pierced the hull of the ship, they gasped for oxygen. After a big explosion, they could feel the heat of the fire on their skin.

Samir and Majid weren't in an auditorium at B Happy Land any more. They were tumbling helplessly into the heart of a blazing inferno. The molten mass spun, then grew dimmer and changed into a giant black and white spiral. The two boys were being swallowed up in an abyss, without beginning or end.

The B Max auditorium fell silent again. Eddie quickly examined them. They'd been mesmerized by the long computerized sequence, and the SuBtle Hypnosis black and white spiral had met with no resistance at all. They were now in a deep hypnotic state, eyes wide open.

"Majid, can you hear me?"

"Yes."

"Samir, can you hear me?"

"Yes."

Eddie glanced up at the dark room where Orwell was hidden. The interrogation could begin.

Eddie received his instructions from Orwell through an earpiece. The two men had agreed to start with a series of simple questions, designed to test how the kids behaved when they were telling the truth.

Majid declared he was called Majid Badach, lived with his mum and dad in Hummingbird Tower on the Moreland Estate, would soon be thirteen and was starting Year 9 next year. While Samir provided similarly straightforward answers, Orwell checked out the equipment up in the projection room.

The children's reactions were recorded by broken lines on long strips of paper. The armbands they were wearing measured their blood pressure.

The wire tied around their chests relayed their respiratory rate. The electrodes on their fingers measured how much they were sweating. Now Orwell knew what the lines looked like when Majid or Samir was telling the truth.

He whispered a few words into the microphone. Eddie repeated the question. "Majid, you've got a flash computer, haven't you? How did you get hold of it?"

"I won the Price Shrinkers competition," Majid answered docilely.

"Good, good … and this computer, is it still in your flat?"

"No."

"Where is it now?"

"At Hugh's."

"Hugh's? Who is Hugh?"

"You know, my English teacher."

"Ah! And what is his full name?"

"Hugh Mullins."

"Very good."

Eddie listened to Orwell's voice and then carried on. "Samir, do you know who Sven is?"

"No."

"Let me try and refresh your memory. Sven was found dead in the basements of Hummingbird Tower. Are you with me?"

Up on high, in front of his graphs, Orwell saw that Samir's heart was beating faster. The lines were rising in peaks, indicating that the kid was experiencing a strong emotion.

"Yes," admitted Samir.

"Sven had a mobile phone. Do you know what happened to it?"

"I … I found it."

"Did you keep it?"

"Martin … she confiscated it off me."

"Who is Martin?"

"Nadia Martin. She's our science teacher."

"Perfect. Samir, did you kill Sven?"

"No!" Samir was wriggling about, as if trying to free himself from the straps securing him to his seat.

"All right," said Eddie. "It wasn't you. Do you know who *did* kill Sven?"

Up in the projection room, Orwell noticed the question plunged Samir into violent turmoil. He ordered Eddie to repeat it.

"I … I don't know."

"Push it!" Orwell shouted.

"Samir," said Eddie patiently. "Even if you don't know for sure, maybe you've got an idea. Can you try and guess who killed Sven?"

The lie detector was going frantic.

"Was it Hugh? Was it Albert?"

"No!"

"Come on, you must have an idea."

"Joke," whispered Samir. "I think … Joke…"

Eddie glanced up at the projection room. "Who's that? Who is Joke?"

"He's the golem … he escaped from the game."

Eddie felt a shiver run down his spine. Orwell was still examining his graphs. With a tense smile, he saw that the kid was calm again. It hadn't been easy for him to tell the truth.

But it *was* the truth.

The Little Girl
with the Windmill

Sebastian and Aisha had wolfed down half their enormous pizza. But, as time ticked by and there was still no sign of Samir and Majid, each mouthful became more difficult to swallow.

"My dad said—" Aisha started again.

"I know." Sebastian scanned the crowds of people swarming around the Mega B Café.

Three tables away, a little girl was tucking into an ice cream with a big dollop of whipped cream on top. She was holding her spoon in one hand and a toy windmill with black and white plastic blades in the other. Sebastian wondered if he'd fancy an ice cream after his pizza. "Let's give it another fifteen minutes," he decided, "and then we'll go and see what's happening at the B Max."

Back at the B Max, the session was over and the lie detector's verdict was clear: the kids weren't lying. This Joke of theirs really did exist. Which meant everything else was starting to look like it might be true too. Bernard Martin-Webber claimed he'd seen a horde of beasts with horns, fur and feathers rampaging through Moreland Town. And Eddie had provided a similar description.

A description of the Evildoers.

Albert's game appeared to be capable of spewing out its characters onto the streets. It was incredible. It was extraordinary. There was just one problem.

It was impossible.

I need Albert, thought Orwell. I need him alive. The boys had talked about him. He was hiding out in some kind of camper van. But neither Samir nor Majid knew what make of vehicle it was, far less its registration number. It belonged to Sebastian's parents. So the information would have to be got out of Sebastian.

A niggling voice inside Orwell kept saying:

A golem escaping from the game, that's impossible … impossible … impossible… But, according to its inventors, it was also impossible to cheat the SuBtle Hypnosis system. So he decided to try one final test.

In the auditorium, Eddie was pleased to see that both Samir and Majid were in a state of deep sleep. They would only wake up when given the order. And they'd have forgotten everything. Incredible, this SuBtle Hypnosis business. He gave a start as Orwell loomed behind him.

"Take a seat, Eddie."

"Me, Mr Orwell?"

"I'd like you to undergo a little hypnosis too."

"Me, Mr Orwell?" There was a hint of reluctance in Eddie's voice. SuBtle Hypnosis was incredible – on other people. He'd heard about the possible side effects and wasn't too keen on being used as a guinea pig.

"You *are* going to cooperate, aren't you, Eddie?" whispered Orwell. "Focus on the black and white spiral. It won't take long. I've just got one little question to ask you.

"Eddie, did you really see the Evildoers in Moreland Town?"

Back at the Mega B Café, Aisha was getting impatient. "OK, shall we go?"

Sebastian had gone for the ice cream with whipped cream on top. "Fwee minith," he mumbled, his mouth full.

Aisha sighed and, with her cheek resting on her hands, dreamily watched the girl with the windmill. She was thinking of her little sister. Aisha wasn't always happy at home, but she was missing her family already.

Suddenly she shrieked. An old lady in a black dress and a black hat had just popped up beside her, blocking out the sunlight. A horrible old lady.

"Don't be frightened, my child," the old lady croaked in a falsetto. "Don't you recognize me? I'm B-Witched. I know everything there is to know about the past and the future. Don't you want to discover your destiny?"

"No!" Aisha cried.

"What about you, young man?" B-Witched asked Sebastian.

"You shouldn't mess around with that kind of stuff," he warned. "Witchcraft's a serious business."

"And I'm dead serious. Hold on, maybe I can convince you. Give me your hand."

Sebastian giggled and held out his hand.

"Ooooh!" said B-Witched. "I see you've come from another land. Near the capital, I think?"

Sebastian shrugged, refusing to let this impress him.

"You like nature a lot."

"Er…"

"I mean, your *parents* love nature."

"Yeah, *they* do!"

"I can see you … how peculiar … you're in a house, but a house on wheels."

Sebastian burst out laughing. "That's the camper van! How did you guess?"

"I know everything, my child. I … my eyes aren't as good as they used to be … I can't read what make it is. I can see the logo, but…"

"It's a VW."

"Yes, that's right. When I was younger, I could have read the number plate. I can see a 4, I think, but … ah … it's all going hazy now. My poor eyes are worn out. Can you help me?"

"P476," Sebastian began.

Just then they were joined by the little girl who'd eaten the ice cream. Still clutching her black and white windmill, she plonked herself right in front of B-Witched. "You're not even a real one," she proclaimed. "First of all, there's no such thing as witches."

B-Witched tried to brush her aside. But the kid wasn't giving up. "It's like those Father Christmases in the shops. They just want to get you to pay for a photo with him. It's a load of rubbish."

"Clear off, or I'll cast a spell on y... A spell... A sp..." B-Witched's voice was stuck.

"See! See! You don't dare!" crowed the little pest.

B-Witched had turned into a statue. Her dilated pupils were fixed on a specific point: the windmill. As it turned, its black and white sails made a spiral.

"Admit you're not B-Witched!"

"I am not B-Witched." The witch's voice had changed. It had suddenly gone very deep.

A man's voice.

"Wow! You're not even a girl! Go on, admit it, you're a boy, aren't you?"

"I am a boy."

"What's your real name?"

"Eddie."

Eddie was having a hypnotic relapse.

"So why are you dressed up as a witch?"

"I'm carrying out my mission."

"Really?" The little girl looked interested. "What kind of mission?"

"I've got to track down Albert. I've got to make Sebastian talk."

Sebastian, who'd been watching what was going on, stood up suddenly. "What? What have you got to make me talk about?"

"The camper van."

"The camper van?" he echoed. "What d'you want to know about it?"

"Its registration … registration…"

"Number," Sebastian finished off.

"Wow, sounds like an exciting mission!" The little girl laughed scornfully.

Sebastian grabbed Aisha by the arm. "Come on. We've got to get out of here." He bumped into the little girl on his way to the exit, knocking the windmill and bringing the hypnosis to an end.

Eddie shook himself, wobbled and then collapsed in the middle of the Mega B Café, all tangled up in his big witch's dress.

"What's going on?" he whispered.

By the time Eddie came round, his prey was already far away. Sebastian was running across the theme park, dragging a disorientated Aisha by the hand.

"Aren't we going to the B Max?"

"Hurry up!"

"But we can't leave the others!"

"Faster, Aisha!"

"Tell me what's going on!" Aisha broke free and burst into tears.

"We've fallen into a trap," said Sebastian. "I'm sure of it."

"What about Majid? And Samir?"

"Prisoners. Come on, let's get going."

They started running again.

"Sebastian, where are we going?"

"We've got to get out of here."

Aisha stopped at the entrance to FunLand, out of breath, and refused to go any further.

"Come on," he urged. "We'll hide in the human body." He dragged her towards the staircase that led to the giant white teeth.

"Why did Eddie tell us everything?" Aisha wondered, standing on the tongue. "People don't tell when it's a trap."

Crouched down in the oesophagus, Sebastian said, "There was something funny about Eddie. Let's sit in the stomach for a bit. I've got to think this one through."

The stomach wall palpitating behind them made a dull thudding noise. Sebastian was trying to collect his thoughts, piecing the story together out loud.

"Maybe Eddie was trying to warn us … maybe he's a friend of Albert's. Albert's a sort of secret agent who … who's recruited Nadia Martin. They've turned the camper van into their base. I should have suspected something when B-Witched asked me about the camper van. I'm such a fool! But when she turned into Eddie… Aargh, man!"

"What?"

"I just don't get it."

Alias Has a Mind
of Its Own

"Wicked!" cheered Majid. "I thought we were dead."

"That giant meteorite trashed us!" crowed Samir. "What was the ending again? Wasn't there some rescue thing, like in *Titanic*? And what's with the BIT *Starship*? It didn't get brucked too, did it?"

They couldn't remember anything after the giant explosion that had interrupted the B Max session.

"Who's that?" Majid had just noticed the smiling stranger to the right of his chair.

Orwell was gloating. Just as he'd hoped, every trace of the interrogation under hypnosis had been erased from the children's minds. "I'm ... the projectionist," he improvised. "There was a small technical hitch. I'm afraid you missed the ending. But rest assured: against all odds, the captain of the BIT *Starship* makes it into hyperspace and brings the team back safe and sound to the astroport at BIT City."

"Over nang!" said Samir.

"It's mad," muttered Majid. "I remember being dead, my face getting smashed to pieces, and then…" He frowned. Something was missing. Like a black hole. He felt uncomfortable and a bit sick. Not surprising, really. This morning he'd nearly puked in the helicopter. So outer space…

"What about that other guy?" Samir wanted to know. "Where did Eddie go?"

"He'll be back," Orwell assured them. "He went to stretch his legs. He knows the B Max movies by heart."

Just then a voice boomed out from the back of the auditorium, near the entrance. "They got away!"

It took Majid and Samir a moment to recognize the strange creature rushing up the aisle towards them. Eddie's pointy hat was hanging off one ear and he was trailing a black dress behind him, waving his arms about, trying to extricate himself.

"I don't know what hap—"

"We'll sort that out later," interrupted Orwell. "Go and tidy yourself up."

"Look, I've got to explain. You're not going to believe me. The spiral came back."

"That's an order, Eddie!"

"There was a little girl with her windmill – are you following me? Next to that kid, Sebastian."

Majid and Samir looked at each other, intrigued. Eddie was totally off his rocker.

"Be quiet!" roared Orwell.

Eddie staggered a few steps before collapsing onto a chair. "It's coming back," he moaned. "It's coming back."

There was a sound like a train being derailed in his throat, and then he declared in a falsetto, "I know everything there is to know about the past and the future. Don't you want to discover your destiny?"

"Eddie! Eddie!" growled Orwell threateningly.

Speaking in his normal voice again, Eddie vowed, "I'll tell the truth. The whole truth.

Nothing but the truth. I'm a man. I'm carrying out my mission. I've got to track down Albert. I've got to make Sebastian talk."

Orwell went up to Eddie and shook him hard. In the background, Samir and Majid were getting restless.

"What's going on?"

"He said he's got to find Albert."

Orwell came over, arms outstretched like a mother hen spreading her wings to gather her little chicks. "Eddie, hey?! He's hilarious in his witch's outfit!" he said, forcing his mouth into a big smile.

A horribly big smile.

"He said something about Albert," said Majid accusingly.

"No, no, not Albert," Orwell corrected him. "*Sherbet*. He thought it tasted like sherbet."

"What?" asked Samir.

"What?" echoed Orwell. "Well … er … the wine. He thought the wine tasted like sherbet. Eddie's an excellent guide and he's a hilarious witch, but he drinks. There you go. I didn't want to tell you, but it's the sad truth. He drinks."

"The truth!" bawled Eddie.

Majid glanced at his watch. A wave of panic washed over him. How come they'd been in the B Max so long? "Where are Sebastian and Aisha?"

"They've escaped," Eddie blurted out. "I've failed. That's the truth."

Orwell turned on him furiously. "Be quiet, you drunkard!"

"I have to tell the truth, otherwise the spiral will come back."

Orwell looked like he was about to do some criminal damage to Eddie. But he needed to reassure the children first.

"Let us out of here!"

"Where are they? Aisha! Sebastian!"

Orwell realized it was going to be very difficult. And it wasn't a job he was suited to, either. He'd been making people feel insecure for years. He watched the two kids running between the chairs towards the green rectangle where the word EXIT shone out of the gloom.

"It's locked," he called out to them. "There's an electronic locking system."

He let them drum against the heavily padded door for a while.

"Open up! Open up! We want to get out!"

Orwell pulled a sad face. "But you've won a whole weekend at B Happy Land. Are you bored already? Your visit's not over yet."

He let a few seconds tick by while he pretended to think the matter over. "How about a little trip? Have you ever been to Gruyères?"

Fifteen miles away, not far from the quaint town of Gruyères, was the most secure building in the world: the headquarters of the Big B Corporation. In the heart of this blockhouse was a small concrete room that didn't feature on any map, a secret meeting place bristling with hidden cameras, bugging devices and detection traps.

Security. This was the theme of the meeting being held there today. Because in the most secure building in the world, security was no longer guaranteed. Mr William was chairing the meeting. Those who only knew him as a cruel and capricious buffoon would have been astonished to see him now: nervous and anxious. He wasn't himself when Orwell was absent. The minutes kept ticking by, and still no sign of his personal assistant.

Mr William was observing his new head of security, Calvin Muller. The son of the number one supplier of Swiss safes, Muller had worked at the Pentagon for a couple of years. He knew a thing or two about surveillance systems. But right now he was stumbling over his words, trying to play down the seriousness of the situation.

"We're making headway," he said. "Once again, we've experienced a few incidents we haven't yet got to the bottom of, but I think we're on the right track. The system will soon be one hundred per cent under our control. And I'd like to reiterate that HQ security is more than satisfactory."

Mr William exploded.

"Satisfactory!" he roared. "D'you know what Alias stands for? Artificial Logical Intelligence for Absolute Security. *Absolute* security, Muller! I've sunk a fortune into that system. I demand absolute security!"

Calvin Muller took a handkerchief out of his pocket and dabbed his upper lip, which was moist with sweat. "The Alias system is the most high performance in the world. But that's also why it's … er … very complicated," he mumbled. "And unfortunately my predecessor, Mr Granter, didn't know how to control it properly."

Mr William glanced at his watch. An enormous watch with a pink strap and Beautiful B lifting her skirt flirtatiously on the face.

What on earth was Orwell doing?

Orwell wasn't far away. Barely two hundred metres from the secret meeting room, as it happened. A few minutes earlier he'd made it through double-entrance security door number 8, with Samir and Majid. Two guards drafted in from B Happy Land escorted the two outraged kids. Badach and Ben Azet had bellowed in protest the whole trip. Orwell couldn't get over their rich vocabulary. To tell the truth, he didn't know what some of the words meant.

"Where are we?"

"What you gonna do with us?"

The two kids looked around them in amazement.

"Why've they all got guns?" Majid wanted to know.

At B Corp HQ you couldn't take ten paces without tripping over an armed guard. Ever since Alias had started showing signs of weakness, all the posts had been doubled up.

"It's the Swiss army barracks," guessed Samir.

"Exactly," Orwell agreed. He clicked his fingers at one of his men. "Take our young friends to the Swiss army nursery," he ordered. He gestured apologetically at his reluctant guests. "I've got to leave you now. A meeting. We'll see each other later. Be good."

The guard at the exit to double-entrance security door number 8 didn't budge. He had a sheepish look on his face.

"Come on, what are you waiting for? Open up!"

"Sorry, sir. The door won't unlock any more. I'm sorry, sir."

"Try again!"

The guard pointed his smart card towards the lock. "This has happened before," he said. "We're having more and more security problems, sir. There we go, I think that's it."

A click signalled that the door was opening. An alarm immediately started up.

"That's the fourth time today, sir."

"Turn that thing off!"

"Right away, sir." The guard rushed over to a control panel and pressed three buttons. Nothing happened. "I've got to shut off the mains supply," he declared.

"Well, get on with it, then!"

"Zone 43 will no longer be protected by Alias, sir."

"I don't care. Turn it off!"

The security guard pulled a lever. The alarm cut out.

"We've got one minute and thirty seconds to vacate Zone 43, sir."

"What?"

"This area will be sectioned off. If we stay here, we'll be locked in. It might take several hours to open it up again."

"Wretched system!"

Samir and Majid glanced at each other: they were tempted to put up a fight. But the guards surrounding Orwell pointed their guns threateningly. They were following instructions in the event of Alias being temporarily out of service. Samir and Majid forgot the urge to rebel.

"Come on. Hurry up!" ordered Orwell.

They rushed down the sinister corridor bathed in orange light that led away from security door 8. At the other end the black metal bars had been raised.

"Take the staircase!" said the security guard. "The lifts for 43 are out of order."

Majid and Samir ran up the steps, jostled by elbows and guns. The guards' boots rang out in the concrete stairwell behind them.

Orwell was the last to reach the west wing. It was deserted. The evacuation procedure had emptied it of all employees. A detection device flashed on the ceiling. Three identical nozzles with beaked tips emerged from a trap. They doused the middle of the room in a mountain of foam.

Orwell grabbed the security guard by his dripping sleeve. "Can you explain this?"

"No, sir. The fire alarm's been set off. But I don't understand how it happened, sir. First of all there's no fire. Plus Zone 43's been cut off. It's as if Alias is operating even when a zone's out of its control. I'd say this is a major incident, sir."

"Yes," said Orwell, getting his breath back. "I'd say so." He brushed the foam off his clothes. His eyes fell on the children. Majid and Samir were clinging to one another, terror-stricken. "Somebody look after them!" he shouted. "Give them a hot chocolate and some dry clothes." Quietly he growled, "Unless Alias controls the hot drinks machine too."

Orwell didn't waste time changing. Dripping from head to toe, his hair white with the remains of the foam, he went into the meeting room and sat down opposite Mr William. His fat boss stared at him.

"Is it raining, Orwell?"

"My apologies for being late, Mr William. Could you tell me where you've got to?"

"Mr Muller was telling us about the weaknesses in the Alias system. Unfortunately, he has nothing new to say on the subject."

Calvin Muller was deathly pale. He was flicking through his paperwork, trying to disguise the fact that his hands were trembling.

"Zone 43 has been cut off," Orwell informed him. "An alarm was set off for no reason. Then the anti-fire nozzles were activated, even though the area had been isolated. I think we're going to have to rename the system. Artificial Logical Intelligence doesn't fit the bill any more. We'll replace Artificial with Autonomous. Alias is no longer obeying orders."

"Admit it!" whined Mr William. "Admit you've lost control of the system. The enemy has infiltrated us! We're at their mercy!"

"I wouldn't go that far," stammered Muller.

The head of security's fear was palpable. Most people responded to Mr William's tantrums in this way. But, watching him, Orwell realized that Muller wasn't scared of the fat man. Muller was terrified of the situation.

Muller was terrified of Alias.

"We want the truth," Orwell said levelly. "What exactly is going on, Mr Muller?"

"I … I don't know," Muller finally admitted. "Each time we think we've solved a problem, another one crops up. It's very strange. It's like Alias is toying with us, teasing us."

"Is it being tampered with from outside?"

Muller shrugged. "By who? And how? I've thought of that, of course. But I can see only one possibility: Granter. Maybe he kept a few key secrets to himself, affording him remote access to the system. But let me remind you that these incidents started before he left his job. He was having difficulties controlling his own creation."

"It's a conspiracy!" howled Mr William. "We're being attacked from all sides. They're spreading evil rumours about B Corp on the Net. They're plotting our downfall!"

Orwell ignored this outburst. "Mr Muller," he said, "I'm giving you a fortnight to get a security system up and running that's one hundred per cent efficient. And I'm talking one hundred per cent safe, one hundred per cent controllable." And when you've done that, old boy, he thought, I'll have you buried with your secret in the bowels of HQ. Like in the good old days of the Pharaohs.

But in order to get the situation properly under control, he needed to get his hands on Albert. And to get his hands on Albert, he needed to find that kid who was running around B Happy Land.

What was his name again?

Sebastian

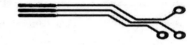

Before hurtling down the intestinal toboggan together, Sebastian explained his plan to Aisha. Then, as soon as the giant human body had expelled them with its disgusting sound effects, they raced over to the nearest B Gifted shop. Sebastian bought two farting goo hats, a Fit B moustache and a pair of Beautiful B pink sunglasses. Once they were both kitted out, they headed in the direction of the main exit.

"Don't run," he ordered, tugging at Aisha's arm.

"But it's miles away!" she groaned.

"If we rush, they'll spot us straight away. The main thing is to keep a lookout for spies."

Aisha agreed: they must avoid all Bumper Birds and My Little B Ponies.

"Oh, no!" He had just realized that the only way of reaching the exit was via ComputerLand with its maze of mirrors and screens. All around them, in different shapes and sizes, face on and in profile, flat and in 3D, black and white and in colour, countless distortions of Sebastian and Aisha kept popping up.

"Wedge your hat on and keep your head down," he muttered without unclenching his jaw.

In fact, their picture had been registered and transmitted to headquarters when they were in the B Gifted shop. And now four Bumper Birds, three Big B Teddies and a My Little B Pony were all converging on ComputerLand...

The children thought they were safe when they got to ConsumerLand. The way it had been decorated reminded them of the Big B Stores in Moreland Town. But twenty times bigger. The boxes of Big B choco-pops up on the shelves were one and a half metres high and the bottles of Big B cola held twelve litres.

"How do people manage?" Aisha wondered. "There's no way you'd get those boxes in your trolley!"

"That stuff's not for sale, you silly—" Sebastian stopped. He didn't want to hurt Aisha's feelings. In fact, given half a chance, he'd have said something very different. It felt good, being alone with her. The danger added to the excitement. He was the one taking charge. Aisha followed him. She obeyed him. Maybe she even quietly admired him.

"There! Look!"

Aisha had caught sight of a My Little B Pony's blue mane. The ridiculous furry animal was at the far end of an aisle that seemed to go on for ever, stacked with Big B products. To avoid it, the children turned off after a pile of Beach B crab sticks. There were dozens of electric shopping trolleys lined up in front of them.

"Get in!" ordered Sebastian.

They climbed into one of the trolleys and tore down an aisle of Baby B food tubs.

Bad idea. My Little B Pony and Bumper Bird popped up at the first intersection. My Little B Pony was over two metres tall. Bumper Bird was skinny as a rake, trailing a long feathery tail. Hooves and claws reached out to grab them.

"Seb! Turn!" Aisha pleaded.

On both sides giant jars of Fruity B jam and Busy B honey rose up in great pyramids. The trolley veered to the right. The shelves were protected by aluminium posts linked by red tape. Instinctively Aisha and Sebastian both lifted the tape as the trolley hit the fragile barrier.

Pots and jars came crashing down. Sebastian nearly passed out when a kilo of apple purée landed on his farting goo hat. Aisha got away with the contents of a cardboard tub of "honey from various flowers" dripping all over her shoulder. Bumper Bird and My Little B Pony were half buried near by. By the time they'd unstuck themselves from the sticky pulp dripping from mane and crest to hooves and claws, the alarm had gone off and a crowd came rushing over from every aisle of ConsumerLand.

Sebastian and Aisha pelted down a long aisle, leaving a trail of sticky footprints behind them.

"Come on!" Sebastian called, chucking away his farting goo hat and fake moustache.

"Then what?" panted Aisha. "Where are we

going? I don't even know where Switzerland is."

Sebastian didn't answer. He could see the giant arches that led out of B Happy Land. That was all that mattered for now.

Three security guards awaited them in front of the barriers. Sebastian was ready to put up a fight.

"Stamp?" asked one of them.

"Sorry? What?"

"I need to stamp your hand, otherwise you won't be able to get back in today," explained the man in slow careful English.

"It's OK. We're not coming back."

They were free. On the other side the queue of visitors stretched over a hundred metres.

"Seb! Seb! Where are we going? I don't want to go to Switzerland."

They were approaching the car park: a sea of vehicles stretching as far as the horizon.

"We've got to find somebody," said Sebastian. "Maybe a policeman who speaks English?"

But how were they supposed to find one of those? They headed towards the cars: there were Volvos, Peugeots, Fiats, Renaults, Toyotas. People stared at them. They were quite a sight, faces smeared with jam and clothes covered with multi-coloured streaks.

"I don't believe it." Sebastian had come to a complete standstill. "It can't be."

"What?" Aisha asked hopefully.

"Over there. That big white thing. The VW."

It was sticking out above the car roofs like an upside-down ship riding the metal waves.

"What is it?"

"A camper van. The same as my parents. I don't believe it!"

They headed over, hesitantly at first but then running faster and faster. The white camper van stood out a mile. His heart pounding, Sebastian tried to make out the registration number. P ... 4 ... 7 ... 6.

"It's our van!" he shouted. He threw himself at the door. It was locked. He started drumming frantically on the side. "Open up, it's us! Sebastian and Aisha! Open up!"

A few seconds went by and then they heard a noise coming from inside the van. The door opened.

And Sebastian came face to face with the most beautiful woman he'd ever set eyes on. A blonde with pneumatic curves and a crystal-clear gaze, a dream babe in shorts and a strappy top.

Things could have been worse, he reckoned. He could have died staring at something ugly.

Because the stunning woman was pointing a deadly weapon at him. And there was no mistaking the expression on her face.

She was about to use it.

Investigator

Orwell hadn't wasted a second. Before leaving B Happy Land, he'd made contact with Constantin Lupescu, the man in charge of the Investigator system. He'd provided Lupescu with the two names extracted from the children during the hypnosis session at B Max: Hugh Mullins and Nadia Martin. And he'd given him one clear and simple instruction: "I want to know *everything* there is to know about them."

Lupescu had two hours in which to make Investigator deliver. Investigator was a branch of Alias, a sort of pathologically curious Sherlock Holmes.

Everything, Orwell had said. And now he was starting to regret it. Seated in a small leather armchair in the middle of the data-processing centre at B Corp HQ, he watched the information unfurling. It was coming through at a dizzy pace on the five screens in front of him, before being rattled out at an infernal rate from the printers.

Orwell grabbed a sheet at random. It concerned the 1996 National Schools Athletics Competition. One hundred metres sprint final. First place: Nadia Martin. "Fascinating." He turned to Lupescu. "Constantin, sort this lot out. I want a breakdown in fifteen minutes."

"You wanted to know everything, Mr Orwell," pointed out Lupescu, smiling sarcastically.

"Mullins is the one who interests me most. Who is this guy? What does he spend his money on? Does he do drugs? Has he got a girlfriend?"

Lupescu indicated that he'd understood.

Fifteen minutes later, he knocked on the door of office 000 on Level -2.

"I'm all ears," announced Orwell.

In a neutral voice, Lupescu started reading the summary he'd prepared. "Mullins lives with his mother in a two-bed flat in the suburbs. The mother's a widow, and works as a psychologist. Mullins is an English teacher in a priority education zone, in a secondary school with a 'challenging' reputation. Nadia Martin teaches combined sciences in the same school."

"Is Martin his girlfriend?"

Lupescu shrugged. "I've haven't got anything on that."

Orwell snatched the two pieces of paper Lupescu was holding out to him. All the essential information was there: date and place of birth, family details, qualifications and so on. Each piece of paper had a copy of a passport photo in one corner. Orwell got out a magnifying glass to examine the poor-quality reproductions. "Pretty ordinary, wouldn't you say?"

"The girl's not bad-looking," said Lupescu.

Orwell agreed. "What's the inside story on Mullins? Has he had any trouble with the law?"

"He was arrested in March 1999 following a Reclaim the Streets demonstration."

Orwell smiled. "I see. A pacifist. An anti-globalist."

"Maybe," said Lupescu. "Mullins regularly signs petitions circulated on the Net. Against the death penalty in the US, against—"

"There you go," interrupted Orwell, "he's a pacifist with a big heart. They're our worst enemies, Constantin."

"He gives regularly to television appeals like Children in Need."

"Has he any hobbies or vices?"

"I think we're dealing with a rather dull personality here. He hasn't left Moreland Town for the past six months. A study of his last one hundred and fifty banking transactions doesn't reveal much. He buys books and computer games."

"Ah!" said Orwell.

"His mother's a regular customer at Big B Stores," Lupescu went on. "Buys lots of free-range chicken."

Orwell signalled to him to get to the point.

"Here's the information about the medication he's been prescribed in the last ten months. Tranquillizers, gastric plasters... Mullins is clearly an anxious type." Lupescu pointed to a thick bundle. "That's the list of all his regular Internet correspondents, his favourite sites, plus the contents of his last fifty emails. And here are his last one hundred credit card transactions. Actually…"

Orwell looked up. "What?"

Lupescu wavered a moment. "It's pure guesswork," he said. "The car's in his mother's name. The flat's in his mother's name. He doesn't go out. He plays computer games with twelve-year-old kids. As far as we know, he hasn't got a girlfriend. If you want my opinion, this guy's a repressed homosexual."

"A gay pacifist," muttered Orwell.

"Can I do anything else for you, Mr Orwell?"

Orwell flicked through Hugh's emails. Mullins talked a load of twaddle to his students. He frowned. He'd just realized these infantile exchanges were actually about a game called Golem.

"Very interesting. Thank you, Constantin. Good work!" His eye suddenly fell on the list of credit card purchases. He swore under his breath. "What about that? It's right under your nose, and you didn't notice anything?"

Intrigued, Lupescu had a look. On the first line of the long printout, marked with today's date, was Hugh Mullins's last transaction: 15:53 — B *Happy Land*: 40 *Swiss francs*.

After spending hours queuing to get in, Hugh was now pacing up and down the Big B Way, looking around desperately. How many children were there in this theme park? Five thousand? Ten? Spread out over six imaginary realms, taking up eight hectares of games, attractions, buildings and mazes.

GruyèreLand, ComputerLand, FutureLand … he didn't know where to start.

"This is stupid, totally stupid," he grumbled. "What on earth am I doing here?"

There was no chance of spotting his students in the crowds. But the solution was staring him in the face. Meeting Point. Where all the mums went to be reunited with their kids. I'll get them to make an announcement over the tannoy, he thought. They'd be able to track down the foursome from the Moreland Estate. They were the Big B Stores winners, after all. They must have been given special treatment. The theme park staff would have been briefed. But...

A shiver ran down Hugh's spine. Majid and Samir had walked into a trap, he'd been sure of that from the start. There was nothing to prove they'd been driven to B Happy Land. They might be hundreds – thousands – of miles away.

He shook himself. No. The competition had been organized in broad daylight. Everybody knew Big B Stores had sent the four children to the B Happy Land theme park.

They'll have to get them back safely.

Hugh repeated the phrase to reassure himself. But just as his heart rate was returning to normal, another phrase came into his head.

They could say there'd been an accident.

He tried to laugh it off. Too much imagination, that was his problem.

Why would they do something like that?

He and Albert had had plenty of time to ask themselves this question during their epic journey in the camper van.

"The children are bait," Albert had told him.

"To catch who?"

"Guess!"

Bingo, thought Hugh. I've taken the bait.

He wasn't surprised when My Little B Pony and Bumper Bird closed in on him. They were tall and strange and furry, and they smelt of mothballs. My Little B Pony gripped him with a hoof that opened up like a lobster's pincer. Bumper Bird sneaked a long silky tail around his neck. Neither of them seemed remotely interested in Hugh himself. They were looking at something else, in Bumper Bird's claw.

"OK, it's him all right," came a muffled voice through a padded outfit.

Hugh glimpsed a blown-up copy of his old passport photo, the kind that makes you look like an axe murderer.

"Follow us and don't make a fuss," Bumper Bird ordered. "Or I'll strangle you."

Hugh nodded to show he'd got the message.

If somebody had told him it was possible to kidnap a person from a theme park in full view of ten thousand people, he wouldn't have believed them. But, as he was now finding out, nothing could have been easier. Bumper Bird could have plucked his eyes out and My Little B Pony could have chopped off his arms. People would have laughed and clapped. Life was one big show at B Happy Land.

It was a short journey. A black hood over his head meant Hugh didn't get a chance to admire the countryside. But it wasn't hard to guess where he was being taken. Albert had showed him on a map the road that led from B Happy Land to the small town of Gruyères. There were various options after that. The way you approached B Corp HQ depended on whether you were a straightforward visitor, a low-ranking secretary or the manager of a key department. Hugh knew there was some kind of glass front, an official entrance, with a car park and flashing signs, a main reception, smiles and green plants. But this part of B Corp was just the tip of the iceberg. And, like icebergs, the invisible part was far more important. According to Albert, the bunker had three underground floors, buried in the rock. Hundreds of offices, miles of corridors, hectares of warehouses… Hugh had no doubt he was somewhere in that vast secret domain that never saw daylight. When his black hood was taken off, he saw exactly where: in front of office 000.

The door opened and he got his first glimpse of Orwell.

Hugh was prepared for a violent encounter, but Orwell barely glanced at him. He was sitting at his desk, writing a letter. "Let's not waste any time," he said, still scanning the letter. "I imagine you're a reasonable man, Mullins."

He pressed a button on a remote control. Opposite him, on a CCTV screen, a small anonymous room flashed up. Hugh gasped. Standing helplessly in the middle were Majid and Samir.

"Where are the others?" he whispered. "Aisha? Sebastian?"

"I've got nothing against these children," said Orwell. "Or you, for that matter. You've got caught up in something that's nothing to do with you."

"Your methods are unspeakable! B Corp is—"

"Don't go getting the wrong idea, Mullins. The company I represent isn't the inhuman monster some people like to make out it is."

"Cut the speeches," Hugh muttered. "What d'you want?"

"The location of the camper van. A Volkswagen, if my information is correct."

Hugh was stunned.

"We're not inhuman, but we are determined," said Orwell. "I'm telling you this quite frankly: Mr William would like…" He paused. "Have you heard of Mr William?"

Hugh blinked and Orwell carried on. "Mr William would like a little chat with one of our former employees. You know him by the name of Albert. B Corp would also like to regain possession of an experimental computer. That computer is very important to us. In case you're not aware of the facts, let me remind you that it was stolen."

Hugh's stomach lurched. *Natasha!* He felt vaguely ashamed that the idea of turning in Albert was less painful than the prospect of handing over his computer.

"I … I don't know what you're talking about," he stammered. But his answer came so late it sounded ridiculous.

"Watch them carefully," said Orwell, pointing at the children on the small screen. "Watch…"

Ping! The screen went blank.

"Everybody knows they've gone to B Happy Land!" shouted Hugh. "You're going to have to account for them."

Orwell nodded wearily. "We'll be held responsible, I'm well aware of that."

"Turn that screen back on! I want to see them!" Hugh panicked. "You can't, you can't... B Corp would never survive the scandal."

"An accident, Hugh. A helicopter crash. Nobody would ever detect even the slightest trace of torture on their charred little bodies, I promise you."

They could say there'd been an accident.

"You're crazy! It's impossible!"

Orwell seemed to give the matter some thought. "Impossible? Hmm ... no. But unfortunate, I'll grant you. It would be a very expensive way of doing things. Helicopters don't come cheap, you know, and then we'd have to pay compensation to the families. Or rather, our insurers would. The children's parents would get their hands on a tidy sum."

"Where are Sebastian and Aisha?"

Orwell shrugged. "My dear friend, let's hope they're not already in the helicopter. You'd better hurry up."

"I want to see the children," insisted Hugh. "I won't say a word until they're standing next to me."

Orwell smiled. He knew he'd won: when somebody starts making conditions, they've as good as admitted defeat. No doubt about it, Mullins was going to talk.

Lara and the Cowboys

"Open up, it's us! Sebastian and Aisha! Open up!"

Inside the camper van, Albert and Nadia looked at each other in disbelief. Hugh had only just left, and here he was back already with the children!

Natasha reacted the fastest. She rushed over to the door and opened it. Then, seeing the B Corp logo on Sebastian's *Life is Big B* T-shirt, she aimed her eraser-laser. She had to destroy him.

Peowww!

"No!" shouted Nadia.

Sebastian collapsed. The deadly beam had struck him right in the chest.

"The flask! The flask!" yelled Albert.

They tried to grab one of the first-aid kits hanging from Natasha's belt. The girl-golem spun round to face Albert and Nadia, threatening them with her eraser-laser. There was a small saucepan full of dirty water in the sink. Nadia seized it.

"Make the boy better," she ordered. "Or I'll kill you." She held the pan at arm's length, showing Natasha the water she was about to throw.

"Not water," intoned Natasha. "Not water, not water." She was disorientated. She had to make a choice: either she gave life back to B Corp and kept her own, or she let B Corp die but got killed in the process.

"My mission is to destroy B Corp."

"But that's not B Corp, it's a child!"

"A little human," added Albert imploringly.

Outside on the ground, Sebastian was howling in agony. The wound was deep.

"Hurry up," ordered Nadia, "or I'll disconnect you!"

She shook the saucepan, making the water lap round the sides.

"Sebastian is your friend. He's a little human." Albert spoke with quiet desperation. "He's a friend of Hugh's. For God's sake, d'you understand what we're saying?"

"My mission … my mission is…" Natasha stopped. Whatever passed for her brain seemed to be out of action. But, contrary to Nadia and Albert's expectations, she slung the eraser-laser over her shoulder and unhooked one of the flasks. Then, in a voice that sounded almost natural, she said, "My mission is to look after the little human."

Sebastian was about to die. He'd blacked out from the pain. Aisha was standing in front of him crying, speechless with horror. She got another shock when she saw the girl-golem heading their way.

"No," she whimpered, protecting her heart with her hands.

Without realizing it, Aisha was hiding the B Corp logo on her T-shirt, which was just as well. Natasha ignored her. She leant over Sebastian and tipped the flask over his wound. A few splashes of light trickled from its neck.

Sebastian groaned, raised a hand to his forehead, opened his eyes and called out in alarm, "Watch out, she's armed!"

"We're here, Sebathian," said Nadia. "You're out of danger. Get up. D'you feel all right?"

All traces of the wound had disappeared. Sebastian stood up.

Nadia suggested everybody should hide in the camper van and talk about what had been happening. She turned round and gave a cry of surprise. Albert was coming out of the van holding the pan of water. Her cry alerted the girl-golem.

"Smart move," said Albert furiously. His idea had been to douse Natasha while her back was turned. Now they eyed each other warily. It was a question of who would draw first. Natasha gripped the belt of her eraser-laser. She didn't have the weapon in her hand any more, so Albert had a slight advantage. But if he messed up, he knew what to expect.

"Let's ... let's make peace," pleaded Nadia. Her voice shook. "We're friends."

"Alias is my master and Calimero is my ally," replied Natasha.

She didn't look all there. Perhaps this was the moment to get rid of her. Albert tried his luck and chucked some water at her. But the girl-golem leapt to one side with lightning agility.

"Try again," she said.

Albert glanced at the saucepan. It was almost empty. Without much conviction, he aimed at Natasha a second time. And missed.

"Game over," she declared.

But once again her reaction was unexpected. Instead of zapping Albert, she turned and ran off between the cars.

"No!" shouted Nadia. "Come back, Natatha, come back!"

Something that dangerous couldn't be allowed to roam free. Nadia ran after her and Albert followed, both calling out at the tops of their voices, "Come back, come back!" People in the car park watched them go past.

"It's Lara Croft!" cheered one dad. "Go for it, Lara!"

"Nah." His son set him straight. "Lara Croft's got brown hair."

Natasha left a trail of dreams and fantasies in her wake. She soon left Albert behind too.

"Nadia, stop, come back!" He was panting heavily, bent over with a stitch.

But Nadia Martin, the former National Schools

champion, kept up with Natasha's mechanical stride. They left the car park behind them, turned off the road and headed up a mountain footpath.

How long can I keep going? Nadia wondered. Natasha wasn't getting any faster, but she showed no signs of flagging either.

After ten minutes of running uphill, the girl-golem came to an abrupt stop and looked around her. Meadows, cows, mountainside.

Cautiously Nadia approached her, whispering, "Me friend, er … me human…"

What she saw nearly made her shriek in horror. The wind had swept aside Natasha's heavy golden fringe. There was something tattooed on her forehead. No: worse than that. *Engraved* into her flesh. The breeze brought the curtain of hair back down over the four letters.

EMET.

Natasha stretched out her arm and scanned the horizon. "There are millions of levels," she said. She turned towards Nadia, as if explaining it to her. "That is the real world."

"Yeah," panted Nadia.

"Where is Hugh?"

"Thugh?"

"Hugh," Natasha corrected her.

"Yes, Thugh."

"Hugh. Try again."

Nadia sighed and indicated she'd never be able to pronounce it properly.

"Hugh is my friend," chanted Natasha. Then, in a different tone of voice: "My love."

Nadia gave a start. "Your love?"

"I love you, my love," Natasha said without emotion.

"Your love's down there," Nadia informed her. "We've got to get back."

Natasha looked down at the valley. "Back to level one?" Without discussing the matter any further, she did a U-turn.

They'd been walking for ten minutes when Nadia realized the path was following the ridge. They weren't descending any more.

"Natasha, stop! We must have taken a wrong turn. We're lost…"

Down below, Albert was waiting and fuming. He'd been outclassed by two babes. Sebastian and Aisha were sitting on the day seat in the camper van, whispering to each other. Shoulder to shoulder, hand in hand. Danger had brought them together. Sebastian didn't think about whether he was betraying Majid. Albert glanced at them, amused. Then he remembered Nadia and his heart tightened. Was she somewhere on the mountainside, injured, dying?

"And that jerk of a Thingy's not back yet!" he growled. He tweaked aside one of the curtains covering a window and frowned. "What's going on?" He groped for his Beretta.

Out in the car park, surrounded by onlookers, a dozen cowboys were advancing in a semicircle. They were all wearing *Life is Big B* T-shirts under their waistcoats. One of them pulled out his Colt, twirled it a few times and fired it in the air. The others followed suit. A few women squealed. Albert let go of the curtain, spitting "Pile of junk!" Some kind of show for idiots... He didn't notice that the cowboys were slowly closing in on the camper van.

The man wearing a sheriff's star fired at the VW's door and gave it a serious kick. Albert leapt up from his seat and drew his gun.

"Nobody move or you're dead!" the sheriff

declared, bursting in. Two cowboys wrenched the children off their seat, twisted their arms behind their backs and pressed a gun to their heads. "Your weapon," the sheriff ordered Albert.

Outside, the rest of the cowboys were giving a shooting and lassoing demonstration to the sound of deafening *yee-has*. Albert was forced to take the wheel and drive out of the car park. Sitting next to him, the sheriff kept saying hello to the folks outside. Sebastian and Aisha were face down on the floor, their hands tied behind their backs.

The camper van followed the signs for Gruyères. Next stop: B Corp HQ.

Nadia and Natasha reached the car park just as the camper van was pulling away.

"They've gone!" exclaimed Nadia, shocked to see the Volkswagen drive off. She started running, pushing the onlookers aside. "Albert! Wait!"

A hand grabbed her roughly. It was Natasha.

"Danger, B Corp," said the girl-golem, pointing to the cowboys still in the car park.

She raised the eraser-laser. *Click-clack.*

"Go for it, Lara!" cheered a dad.

"That's not Lara." His daughter put him straight. "Lara doesn't have blonde hair."

"Danger, B Corp," Natasha said again.

The hail of gunfire took the B Corp assassins-cum-cowboys by storm. The spectators applauded. *Peowww!* Reload. *Peowww!* Braying like animals, the cowboys arched their backs and collapsed one after the other.

"Wicked! One, two, three in a row!"

There was cheering from all sides. Appalled, Nadia put her hands over her ears. But what she saw was even more horrible than what she tried not to hear. Six bodies writhing in agony.

"Stop! Stop!" She stamped her feet. "Humans! They're humans!"

"Go for it!" roared the delighted onlookers.

Nadia turned to them and shouted, "Get lost, you sick people! She's killing for weal. For weal, d'you understand? For weal!"

A few incredulous laughs greeted her words. Followed by a brief silence. And then panic set in. The surviving cowboys seized the chance to make their getaway, with dads and their little princesses, grannies and grandpas quickly following suit.

Nadia tugged Natasha's arm. "Quick, we've got to heal them. Your first-aid kits, quick!"

But Natasha wasn't having it. "They are bad. I kill bad people."

Of the six cowboys, four had been hit in the head and were lying spreadeagled, their foreheads split open. Were they dead or unconscious? Another was lying on his back, hands clutching his belly, still moving, but only just. Fear had paralysed the last one, who was holding out his arm, unable to get up. Strangely, their wounds weren't bleeding. Instead, a sort of purple flower bloomed around each wound.

"Natatha, please, make them better. Humans. Humans." Nadia knew they were contract killers from B Corp. But this wasn't a funny sequence from a computer game, and there was no screen to shield her from their pain. She had to save them. "Natatha," she improvised, "these are humans. They've got wives and children. They love. 'I love you, my love.' Like Thugh."

"They are bad," insisted Natasha.

"Yes, but bad people can turn out to be nice too. Not in computer games, but in weal life. In the weal world, people can be bad one moment and good the next. D'you understand, Natatha?"

"No."

But she was wavering. Her whole world was wavering. So Nadia took the risk of detaching a flask from the girl-golem's belt. It was light, hardly there. Quickly she ran over to the guy writhing on the ground and poured a few splashes of light over his injured chest.

He was cured in an instant. Picking up the Colt lying on the ground beside him, he aimed it at Nadia.

Peowww! Peowww! Natasha's first laser beam blasted his gun to smithereens, the next went in one side of his head and out the other.

"They are bad," Natasha said again matter-of-factly.

They still had to deal with the guy who'd been hit on the arm. He was young and terrified. The eraser-laser had ripped him open from the shoulder to the elbow, and the invisible scalpel kept on slicing away, making the wound longer and deeper.

"Mercy!" he stammered, seeing Nadia.

"I can save you. But on one condition. I want

to know who gave you your orders and what those orders are."

"I don't know much." He was in such pain he could hardly open his mouth. "We were told to take over the camper van and the people inside it."

"Who gave you that order?" asked Nadia, bringing the flask closer to his wounded arm.

"Mr William. Well, his sidekick, Orwell."

Nadia pretended to pause before tipping the flask. "And where are they taking the camper van?"

"To B Corp HQ. Near Gruyères."

Nadia emptied the healing flask and the wound closed up again.

"That stuff's unbelievable, it's…" The young man was weeping. With terror and relief.

"There's somebody I love in that camper van," Nadia told him. "And two childwen."

"I didn't know. I'm sorry, I really am."

The young man carried on weeping. With terror and regret. When he looked up, Natasha was leaning over him. He thought she was some kind of angel of death and resurrection. "Mercy!" he pleaded again.

"In the real world," she said, "people can be bad one moment and good the next."

Gruyères was ten miles from B Happy Land.

Nadia fastened a holster to her waist, picked up a cowboy hat off the ground and stuck it on her head, signalling to Natasha to follow her. There was nobody around. Panic had emptied the car park.

The two girls took the road that led to B Corp HQ. Nadia was so caught up in her thoughts it took her a while to realize that cars kept overtaking them and, each time, the driver and passengers gave them gobsmacked glances.

"I'm so silly!" she exclaimed. "Let's hitch." She stopped on a straight stretch of road and stuck out her thumb in the direction of Gruyères. Natasha stood next to her, legs apart and hands on hips – a warrior at rest. Nadia had a feeling that, far from disconnecting, the girl-golem was using these down-time moments to absorb new information.

A bright red convertible pulled up alongside them with a screech of tires. The driver was a youngish guy, with a long nose and eyes that were too close together. "Hey girls, fancy a ride?" He flashed them an ultra-bright smile and stroked the back of the passenger seat.

"We're going to Gruyères," said Nadia, deliberately putting on her uptight teacher's voice. "Is it on your way?"

"Course it is, darling," replied the would-be playboy. "What's with the outfits? Good for business, I'll bet." He was ogling Natasha's curves.

"They're fancy-dress costumes. We bought them at B Happy Land," Nadia answered, trying not to groan out loud.

The guy opened his car door and folded the passenger seat forward so Nadia could climb into the back. To his great disappointment, the gorgeous blonde took the back seat and Nadia sat next to him.

"I like the toy guns." He pointed to the Colt and the eraser-laser. And gave a dirty laugh. "I've got one too. Want to see it?"

"We're going to Gruyères," Natasha repeated.

The man set off again, glancing in his rear-view mirror. The babe seemed kind of spaced out. He slammed his foot down hard on the accelerator to impress her. "I'm Stefano. You?"

"I'm Michelle," said Nadia, though he was talking to Natasha, "and she's Bernadette."

"And what are you going to do in Gruyères?" Stefano persisted.

"My mission is to destroy B Corp," responded Natasha.

Stefano burst out laughing. After glancing in the mirror again, he murmured to Nadia, "If they're silicone, they've done a swell job. She must be at least a 38DD!"

Nadia tapped the speedometer. "How about we triple that?"

A Slight Hitch

Orwell cracked the knuckles of his right hand. One by one. He was thinking about Albert. He'd got him. At last. That man had been giving B Corp the slip for months now. But it was finally over. OVER. Orwell had got a call on his mobile: "Operation Cowboy completed. We've got the kids too." Success. Nothing could stop him now. Albert was going to tell Orwell how to make holograms come out of that electric blue computer, whether he liked it or not. The kids would be reconditioned through hypnosis and returned to their parents. Hugh Mullins would end his brief life in a Swiss ravine. There was just the slight hitch caused by the Alias security system, which Calvin Muller had better get sorted as soon as possible.

Orwell checked his watch. The camper van couldn't be far off. All this waiting was making him overexcited. He cracked his knuckles again.

Suddenly a green light started flashing on a huge wall panel depicting B Corp's labyrinthine layout.

"Here they are," he whispered. The flashing light indicated the whereabouts of the camper van. It had just gone through the barrier at the north entrance. He pictured the journey: a stretch of two hundred metres up the mountainside, where an enormous door opened slowly to allow access to the warehouses and garages hewn out of the rock.

The light kept moving. By now Albert should recognize the series of open-plan offices where teams of technicians perfected B Corp products under constant camera surveillance. He'd spent months on end in one of those, inventing and programming Golem.

The light turned red. Albert was getting closer to the holy of holies, the private quarters of Mr William. Then the light went out and Orwell could just hear a faint *beep-beep*. In this most secret of places, there was a darker secret. Those who worked down here never came back out.

Two of these men sworn to the shadows pushed Albert into the room where Orwell was waiting.

"Glad to see you," he sneered, standing in front of his prisoner. "Sorry I can't shake your hand." Albert was handcuffed. "You remember me?"

"We may have crossed paths somewhere," Albert acknowledged. "Aren't you Mr William's housekeeper or something?"

Orwell pretended to find this funny. "Ah!" he said, pricking up his ears. "Talk of the devil..." He could hear the electric buzzing of Mr William's buggy. A heavy curtain parted to let the boss through.

Albert had never seen Mr William before and, for a second or two, he was more curious than afraid. B Corp's boss was a twenty-two-stone monster who went around in a large motorized baby bouncer. His flabby white face resting on a triple chin looked like a custard tart splatted on a plate.

Albert wrinkled his nose in disgust. He wasn't going to be intimidated by a moron and his sidekick. In any case, this kidnapping was madness.

As soon as Hugh realized the camper van was missing, he'd notify the police. All Albert had to do was hold out.

"I haven't heard him squealing in pain," complained Mr William, pointing at Albert.

"We haven't started yet," Orwell answered with a low bow.

"How kind of you to wait for me." Mr William's voice was sickly-sweet.

Albert didn't see it coming. Something struck his face, tearing his cheek and splitting his lip. The shock made him stagger backwards. At the end of Mr William's arm hung a long whip.

Orwell frowned. "Mr William, I've just told you we haven't started the interrogation yet!"

"But I can tell he doesn't want to answer," said Mr William quietly. "He doesn't want to answer because he's proud and plucky." Then he shouted, "And because he hates us! You hate B Corp, don't you?" He raised his whip again and Albert collided with the wall as he tried to dodge.

Orwell gave a little cough to get the situation back under control. "Good, good. I'm sure we can come to an understanding. We've got back the computer you stole, Albert. So there's just one small matter left to sort out, one little thing you're going to do for us and then everybody'll be happy…"

"Maybe we could rip out a couple of nails?" suggested Mr William. "I've noticed that always puts people in the right frame of mind."

Just then, two guards entered and set up the electric blue computer on a table. Orwell rested a hand on the monitor. "Make the characters from Golem come alive for me!"

Albert realized he had to play for time. He gestured to his handcuffs and they were removed. He raised his hand to his mouth, which was filling up with blood, and wiped himself furtively. Then he sat down in front of the computer, switched it on and immediately found the sequence that called up Natasha. The game seemed to be waiting, lurking on the other side of the screen. Albert thought quickly. B Corp knew the characters from Golem could get out of the computer. But Orwell's lack of suspicion must mean that he didn't know how much the holograms had improved, or how hostile they were to B Corp.

Albert typed **Alias**.

Orwell gasped. "What are you doing?" Muller wasn't the only one who was scared of Alias.

"I'm answering the riddle *I am that which is known by another name*," Albert explained.

"Can we cut his ear off too?" suggested Mr William, who was getting bored. It was all taking too long.

Enter your name had just flashed up on the screen. Orwell, who was leaning over Albert's shoulder, typed **Orwell** onto the scroll. The computer went *ting!* and switched itself off.

"He's making fun of us!" shouted Mr William, cracking his whip across Albert's shoulders.

That was going too far. Albert stood up suddenly, grabbed the fat man by the arm and tugged hard, nearly overturning the motorized baby bouncer. The guards raised their guns.

"No, stop!" panicked Orwell. "We need him alive. He's got to talk."

Albert leant against the wall like a prisoner about to be executed.

"And he will talk," Orwell added, "won't he?"

Again Albert wiped away the blood dripping

from his split lip. He said painfully, "This sequence was introduced into my game behind my back. I didn't program it. I don't know what you have to do."

"You're lying! You're lying!" yelled Mr William. "He's lying! He's lying! Rip out his tongue!"

"But Golem is *your* game," said Orwell.

"Yes, it's my game, but it got away from me."

"Got away," whispered Orwell, remembering what Muller had said. "It feels like *Alias* is toying with us, teasing us."

"There's only one man in the world who can make holograms come out of that computer," added Albert, "and I'm not that man."

"He's lying! He's lying!" fumed Mr William. "He's just saying that because he doesn't want us to cut his tongue out."

Orwell shot his boss a look that was far from friendly. In fact it roughly translated as *Shut it, can't you?* He turned to Albert again. "Who? Who can make the holograms come out? I want this man's name."

Albert could have said Thingamabob or even Granter. But he didn't have the presence of mind to lie. "He's called Hugh Mullins."

"Well, what a delightful coincidence!" Orwell exclaimed. "Because guess who's dropped by to pay us a little visit!"

Albert thought his heart was going to stop beating. They'd got Hugh as well! Now he'd *really* put his foot in it. And what about Nadia: was she their prisoner too? Where *were* Nadia and Natasha?

Not very far away. It was 9.15 p.m. and Stefano's red convertible had just reached Gruyères.

"Where are you *really* going at this time of night, girls?"

"To destroy B Corp," said Natasha.

This time Stefano's laugh stuck in his throat. *Totally* spaced out, this chick.

"D'you know where it is?" asked Nadia.

"The … the headquarters of B Corp?" Stefano was getting nervous.

Natasha answered for him. "A mile and a half away. Past the castle, across the Sarine River, take the first right after the bridge."

"She's better than a satellite navigational system," joked Stefano. But his foot was on the brake. He had no intention of taking the girls all the way.

Suddenly he felt something cold pressing against his neck. The eraser-laser.

"Drive!" Natasha ordered.

The hairs on the back of his neck prickled. This wasn't funny any more. He had two anti-globalist terrorists in his car.

"Are you sure about the diwections?" Nadia said, calmly getting her Colt out of its holster.

"Alias is calling me," said Natasha. Her voice sounded robotic again and her eyes had gone blank.

It was 9.20 p.m. Back inside HQ, Hugh had just been taken to his computer. If circumstances had been a little different, he'd have hugged it. For him, it *was* Natasha.

"Make a hologram come out of this computer," Orwell demanded. "Apparently you're the only man who can do it."

Hugh glanced reproachfully at Albert, then felt ashamed. He was the one who'd delivered Albert into B Corp's hands, after all, and now the poor guy's clothes were splattered with blood.

Orwell hadn't finished. "I'm giving you thirty seconds to make up your mind. After that I ... we'll whip Albert again."

"And that's just for starters," Mr William quipped. "We've got lots of little children as well. It's always fun killing little children."

Hugh sized up the situation. The children and Albert had all been taken prisoner. But what about Nadia and Natasha? Where were they? Nobody had mentioned them.

"Now you've only got twenty seconds," said Orwell. "Nineteen, eighteen..."

"No funny stuff," Albert hissed. He was wondering if Thingy had decided to sacrifice him after all.

"Fourteen, thirteen, twelve..."

Hugh took his time. He sat down in front of the computer and stroked the keyboard. If Natasha's back inside, he thought, I can make her materialize here. But how will she react when she finds herself catapulted into the heart of B Corp?

"Is there any water in this room?" he asked dreamily.

"Ten, nine—" Orwell broke off. "No. You can have a drink later!"

No water. The coast was clear for Natasha. Hugh typed his gamer name: **Calimero**.

"Calimero?" Orwell was puzzled.

Hugh stood up and waited for the beam of light to shoot out. But nothing happened.

"He's taking us for a ride!" yelled Mr William. "Calimero? What kind of a crazy name is he going to come up with next? Gouge his eyes out, Orwell!"

OK, thought Hugh, Natasha must still be outside. "It … it doesn't always work," he stalled.

"Well, start again – and you'd better make it work this time," threatened Orwell.

Hugh glanced at Albert to see how he was coping. "You all right?"

"Bearing up," said Albert.

Hugh pulled himself together and typed **Calimero** again.

Orwell had put the counter back to thirty. "Twenty-nine, twenty-eight, twenty-seven…"

Losing his temper, Hugh grabbed the monitor and shook it. He remembered making the Evildoers appear by treating his computer like a cocktail shaker.

"He's gone berserk," objected Mr William. "Hang him by his feet!"

"It works sometimes," stammered Hugh. He collapsed in his chair, disheartened. Then he typed **Calimero** again and whispered, "Natasha…"

9.30 p.m. The huge *Life is Big B* sign was flashing in the dark. Behind the shuttered windows, a feeble glow lit the main entrance hall. The nightwatchman was snoozing at his post. A red convertible was parked in the visitors' car park. Stefano, who kept telling himself he was dreaming, watched the two girls head off.

When the official entrance to B Corp was in her line of sight, Natasha took her eraser-laser in both hands. "Alias is my master and he is calling me."

Peowww! Stefano let out an astonished cry. She'd fired! The blonde had fired! "Help," he whispered. The glass door had exploded. "Po-po-police," he gurgled.

Natasha stepped over the broken glass and entered B Corp. The alarm system wailed. She destroyed the entrance hall with one sweep of her eraser-laser, shattering display windows, paintings and flower pots, and setting fire to magazines, posters and drapes. Finally she stopped firing and walked across the wrecked interior, where the temperature had shot up by fifty degrees in a matter of seconds.

Shell-shocked, Nadia followed in her wake as fake wood beams, shelves and partitions collapsed around them. Behind the reception area and the exhibition rooms dedicated to the glory of B Corp were the offices accessible to the public.

Luckily they were empty.

Orwell froze in disbelief. On the wall panel the zone representing the main entrance to the building had just changed colour. It was glowing bright orange.

"What's going on?" piped up Mr William.

"I don't know. It can't be what I think it is..." Orwell turned to one of the guards. "It's not what I think it is. It can't be ... can it?"

The guard stiffened but didn't say anything.

"What's going on?" roared Mr William.

"Guard," persisted Orwell, "remind us what this means."

"Area destroyed." The man tried to sound as neutral as possible. "Zero security."

Orwell burst out laughing. "That's ridiculous. Area destroyed! We're talking about the main reception."

"Get rid of them," howled Mr William, waving a chubby hand at Hugh and Albert.

"Let's keep calm here," barked Orwell.

But Mr William was panicking. "He typed *Alias*." He pointed accusingly at Albert. "You should have stopped him, Orwell! He can communicate with the system. He wants to drive it crazy! He wants to wipe out our security!"

Orwell frowned. He had a hunch the fat man was right. The orange area on the display panel kept spreading. Then a small red cross lit up.

This time the guard spoke without being asked. "Intrusion through security door 4."

"Impossible!" exclaimed Orwell. Staring defiantly at Albert, he spat, "You know as well as I do, you need an atomic bomb more powerful than Hiroshima to shift that. Nobody can get in there."

Albert shrugged. He'd seen plenty of impossible things recently.

"The reinforcement's half a metre thick," Orwell added.

"All it takes is for Alias to turn the key," Albert replied. "Alias can invite whoever it likes to your place, Orwell."

Mr William let out a scared whimper. Orwell signalled to him to be quiet. "Can you hear something?" he asked nobody in particular.

The squeaking of Mr William's baby bouncer was his only answer. "I'm off. I'm locking myself in my quarters. I've got everything I need to defend myself there."

Albert laughed as the fat man exited. "Half a metre of reinforcement!" he said scornfully. "So how are you going to be able to hear anything, Orwell?"

But Orwell wasn't listening. Up on the wall a new zone had just turned orange. "This is crazy!" he declared. "The thing's gone nuts. Guard, give me your gun."

The guard did as he was told. Orwell fired at the display panel, which exploded in a hail of multi-coloured sparks. He turned to Hugh, grinning broadly.

"Right. Where were we?"

A Game of Massacre

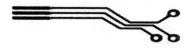

Natasha strode ahead without once looking back. Nadia followed. High up on the metal footbridge they looked down over a world bathed in green light where dozens of glass offices, all identical, were stacked in tiers. At this late hour the cells of the hive were empty.

Nadia imagined it was here, behind one of those glass walls, that Albert had invented his game. Golem. This sinister place was the test tube where the strange creature made out of flesh and electrons, now walking in front of her, had been conceived. Back in her original setting, Natasha was moving with mechanical ease.

Nadia remembered one of Albert's descriptions, and guessed the long corridor off to her left led to the warehouses. He had caused panic at B Corp by hiding the infamous electric blue computer there.

Natasha wasn't interested in the warehouses. She entered what looked like a dead end. There was a dark, shiny barrier in front of her, a wall of steel. No way through. But she refused to turn back. She was brandishing her eraser-laser, which looked like a toy next to the bombproof reinforcement.

Nadia watched the girl-golem's face with astonishment. She looked so attentive, so concentrated, so determined... Suddenly the enormous block of metal started pivoting on an invisible axis, as if she had set it off just by willing it.

The three men on the other side had no time to recover from the shock. Natasha mowed them down, one after the other.

Nadia and Natasha had just entered Mr William's private apartment. Nobody had ever come in this way before. Never, not since the complex was built, had anybody seen the enormous steel wall budge an inch. The secret mechanism only obeyed Alias, and only Alias could authorize it to move once the absolute emergency procedure had been activated.

But of course, nobody had ever activated the absolute emergency procedure before.

After that it was easy. Doors unlocked automatically, bars shot up. And, at every step, guards fell by the wayside.

Orwell hadn't relaxed his grip on the gun. Right now he was aiming it at Hugh. "You saw what happened to the panel. I wonder if your head'll look that pretty when it explodes." He was convinced Hugh was being deliberately obstructive. "If you type in that ridiculous word again, I'll shoot you immediately."

That ridiculous word. *Calimero.*

Albert watched the wimpy teacher. He could tell the poor guy was racking his brains. What was he going to come up with? What else could he type, apart from Calimero? In any case, Natasha was on the loose. Nothing was going to come out of that wretched computer, no matter what they did.

"The children," said Hugh. "I want to see them. Prove they're still alive."

The barrel of the gun pressed against his temple. But Orwell sighed and lowered his weapon. "Very well," he said. "I'll show you the children. You'll see they're doing ever so well. And then you will cooperate."

Hugh felt the barrel of the gun again, like a sliver of ice against his skin, skimming the corner of his eye.

"And you'll cooperate fast," added Orwell. "Otherwise our young friends won't be doing ever so well for much longer."

He switched on the screen showing control room 9. An ugly picture flashed up, grey, run through with white static interference. They could see a few chairs, a table, and that was all.

"Where are they?" asked Hugh.

"I … it looks like they've got out."

"They can't have got out by themselves," said Albert.

Orwell examined the screen, as if he couldn't believe his eyes. "No. They can't have."

For some reason not even he understood, it was taking a while for his anger to erupt.

This time Nadia thought their luck had run out. There were a lot of guards – ten of them. They'd understood they were dealing with a formidable enemy. They were going to have to put their weapons to the test: shoot to kill. Four of them were crouched down, the others stood behind them. They were protecting a gigantic, mysterious wooden door.

Natasha seemed resigned to defeat. She didn't even raise her weapon to fire.

She didn't need to.

Nadia never knew exactly what happened because she buried her head in her hands as the portcullis came crashing down. She heard howling, looked up and saw the men skewered on the pointed bars. The whole front row: all the guards who'd been crouching down. Nailed to the spot. Bleeding.

Nadia thought she was going to pass out. She wanted to block out that monstrous picture, make those death rattles, whimpers and cries of horror stop.

Her wish was granted. A dark cloud enveloped the guards speared by the portcullis, together with those standing behind them. Silence again. They were all on the floor now. Gassed. Wiped out by Alias.

"Alias is my master," said Natasha. Her master and her partner inside the fortress.

The portcullis was raised again, and there was a powerful ventilating noise as invisible pipes sucked up the toxic cloud. Natasha stepped over the bodies and made the colossal wooden door explode.

On the other side was a vast room decorated with murals celebrating B Corp products. High up was a giant tub of fluorescent green farting goo, like some grotesque god of the consumer society.

Natasha aimed her eraser-laser at it and mouthed *"Peowww! Peowww!"* But she didn't fire. Nadia realized she was starting to think before she acted. She didn't fire at objects any more. Just people. And doors.

The last door was the one guarding Mr William's bedroom. Natasha didn't need to blow that to smithereens. It opened of its own accord, with majestic and ironic slowness.

Alias was delivering up its prey.

The noise began straight away, the squealing of an animal facing the slaughterhouse.

"No! No! Not me!" Mr William was cowering in front of a pink four-poster bed topped by a golden crown, in an outsize, ridiculous copy of Beautiful B's bedroom. "Don't shoot me. Look, the children are here. I went to rescue them. I saved them. It's thanks to me. Don't shoot … don't shoot!"

Mr William had abandoned his motorized baby bouncer. He was clutching Aisha to him. Terror shone in her doe-like eyes. Majid, Samir and Sebastian were standing to one side, looking from the fat man to Nadia and Natasha and back again. They didn't know which side they were on any more, or who scared them the most.

"She's just a little girl," Mr William went on. "Come on, you're not going to kill a little girl, are you?" He pressed down on Aisha's shoulders, shook her. "Tell them, go on, you little idiot! Tell them I saved your life!"

Natasha was busy adjusting her aim. She was ready to fire. "Mr William," she said, the soulless dispenser of justice, "I have come to destroy you."

"Mr William doesn't exist!" he shouted wretchedly. "I'm just a clown. I'm a clown…" He tried to shift his position, still gripping Aisha tightly.

"No, Natatha, no," whispered Nadia. "Don't shoot! My God, Aisha…"

"She's going to kill her!" screamed Mr William. "She's going to kill her!"

But Natasha had a mission to accomplish. Her arm outstretched, without trembling, without emotion, she pulled the trigger.

"A clown, a clown," sobbed Mr William. "Orwell's the one you've got to kill! He's the boss!"

Nadia stared at Natasha in amazement. The eraser-laser hadn't worked.

"*Peowww!* Reload," muttered Natasha. She pulled the trigger again. Nothing. She lowered her arm and examined her weapon. A small red bar showed the energy level had dropped to zero.

Mr William laughed like a maniac. "Hee-hee! You can't kill me!"

Natasha fiddled with the eraser-laser, growling, "*Peowww!* Reload." She couldn't understand what was happening. She'd fired a lot and hit a lot of targets. She should have won back loads of energy. What kind of world was this where she couldn't convert her bonus points?

"Let me go," Mr William begged. He was talking to Nadia. Now the danger was less immediate, he released Aisha and took a few pathetic steps towards the young teacher. "I'm just an actor. I'm not the boss of B Corp. Look on the chair. That's my padded belly. I've got false teeth, a wig, stick-on eyebrows. It's all fake. Orwell's the one, he's the real boss of B Corp. I'm just his clown. He's the one you've got to kill. I was being paid to play the villain. I've always liked playing baddies. I've got a talent for it. Nero, Caligulaaaa…" He was sobbing. "Let's get out of here," he said to Nadia. "You can be my queen, my Agrippina!"

Nadia was slowly coming out from under Natasha's spell. In front of her were the four children, her 8D students. This killing had to stop. They had to leave this hellhole. Get out, that was it, they'd got to get out.

Natasha must have sensed Nadia was weakening. With lightning agility, she leapt over to the teacher and ripped the gun out of her hand. A second later, crouching down, both arms extended, she fired.

"Natatha, no!" screamed Nadia.

Mr William toppled backwards onto the bed, hit in the forehead. Nadia rushed over to him, hoping that maybe a magic flask might cure him. Stupid idea. The Colt belonged to a world that was all too real.

"Everything's fake," whispered Mr William. "Everything's fine…"

They were the last words he spoke.

Huddled together, the children couldn't take their eyes off the bloodstain that was spreading over the pretty pink satin bedcover.

"You have twenty minutes to leave the building," recited Natasha. "After that you will be destroyed."

"What?" shouted Nadia.

"You have twenty minutes to leave the building," Natasha repeated in autopilot mode.

Sebastian was the first to pull himself together. "How do we get out of here?" He was looking at his science teacher.

Nadia knew the way back to the reception area:

a path littered with corpses gunned down by a character from a kids' story gone horribly wrong. She turned fearfully to Natasha. "Shall we go?"

"My mission is not complete," answered the girl-golem. She pointed to the four children and added with unexpected tenderness, "Save the little humans."

Since he couldn't find any trace of the children on the screen showing control room 9, Orwell switched on a second monitor. Then a third. And another… The young hostages couldn't be seen on any map, or in any of the rooms they might have been put in. So who had taken the initiative?

Orwell gasped. On the screen for control room 13 he could clearly see, tucked away in one corner, the lifeless body of a man in a uniform.

"Something wrong?" asked Albert.

"Guards!" roared Orwell, addressing the two men on either side of him. "Find out what's happening. I want a summary of the situation in ten minutes."

All the monitors were lit up now. Moving from one screen to the next, a cascade of images flashed before Orwell's eyes as he scoured the bunker at top speed. There were two hundred and twelve cameras in the building.

"What on earth…" He had just seen ten of his men lying in a pool of blood in front of a gigantic wooden door. "An attack!" He turned to Albert, as if he suspected him of instigating it. "I'm going to kill you!" he shouted.

"Keep your wits about you, Orwell," soothed Albert. "You've got twenty minutes left."

"Twenty minutes?"

"You shouldn't have smashed the display panel. It would have kept you updated on the situation." He pointed to something on the screen for checkpoint 7.

"The barrier!" Orwell exclaimed.

"What d'you mean, *the barrier*?" queried Hugh.

"Have you seen any others?" asked Orwell.

"All the barriers are lit up." Albert was calmer than ever. "We're at critical maximum alert."

"What kind of gobbledegook's that?" Hugh wanted to know.

"Evacuation procedure under way," Albert announced. "HQ will be destroyed in less than twenty minutes, if the system isn't deactivated."

Orwell was deathly pale. He stared briefly at the weapon in his hand, as if contemplating murdering his two prisoners. But time wasn't on his side.

"Don't move from here," he barked. "I'm going to the main operations centre to sort out this confounded system. If you take one step outside this room, I promise you I'll … I'll shoot you down like dogs."

Albert shook his head defiantly. "Why are you refusing to face the truth, Orwell? Nobody's set off the maximum alert alarm. You know full well who's controlling the system now. And there's nothing you can do about it."

Orwell looked at him wildly. Then he rushed out into the corridor.

Hugh glanced admiringly at Albert. "You got him to freak out. I hope you can get us out of here before he comes back."

"I think I can find the way."

"As soon as we're out, we'll alert the Swiss police about the missing children."

"Yeah, right," scoffed Albert. "Come on, let's beat it."

After running down a few hundred metres of corridors, Hugh suddenly hesitated. "This maximum alert – you *were* having him on, weren't you?"

"Keep going!"

Hugh felt cold. "It's true? The building's going to be destroyed? But what about the children? We can't abandon them. The children … and my compu— Natasha…"

Albert turned round. "Listen to me. I'm saving my hide. If I can. All we can do is hope Orwell manages to seize control of Alias again. Otherwise this so-called intelligence system is going to blow the whole place up. In approximately fourteen minutes."

"You monster! You'd abandon the children?"

Albert stopped dead. But a sudden apparition saved him having to rack his brains for an answer.

"Watch out!" It was one of the guards Orwell had sent out, staggering back. He grabbed hold of Albert. "It's carnage," he said. "There's corpses everywhere. Please, sir, I want to get out of here."

"Fourteen minutes," Albert said ominously. "If Alias holds out that long."

He set off again at double the speed, thinking the others were following him. But when he turned round thirty seconds later, he could only see the guard.

"Hugh!" he called. "Hugh! You jerk!"

Hugh had set off again in the opposite direction to save the computer, or the children. He didn't know any more. But when he got back to the room where the interrogation had taken place, the computer had disappeared. Orwell must have come back for it, before escaping via some secret exit. He collapsed into a chair. There were just a few minutes left to the final countdown. He was alone in the middle of a maze and he didn't know the way out.

"Mum," he whispered.

Die. He was going to die, far away from the mother he'd never left, far away from Moreland Town, far away from school, far away from everything.

"Hugh."

"Mum?" He looked up and, through a fog of tears, saw Natasha.

"Hugh."

The young teacher stood up shakily. "Are you there? Are you…?" Love made his voice tremble.

It would be all right to die if it was her. But then he remembered his students.

"Natasha, where are the children?"

"With Nadia. Come on."

Hugh took one step but the ground seemed to give way under him. He couldn't take any more. He was going to disappear down a black hole. He felt something closing around his chest, like a vice. Natasha's arms.

"Four minutes," she said.

They hadn't got much time, but they should be able to make it.

Hugh fainted.

When he came to, he was in the B Corp car park, propped against a car. Natasha was crouched down next to him.

"Twenty seconds," she said.

The sound of helicopter blades made him look up. Orwell was making his getaway, and taking the electric blue computer with him.

Hugh didn't get a chance to share this information with Natasha, because she'd started on the countdown.

"Six, five, four, three, two…"

There was a terrifying explosion. Hugh thought the concrete was going to crack open and swallow him up. All the windows came smashing down. Then the walls collapsed.

For one long moment, there was nothing under the moon but a cloud of dust criss-crossed by strange lights.

"Mission completed," said Natasha.

Mission accomplished! But:

DID Albert manage to escape the
exploding bunker in time?

WILL Lulu get out of hospital alive?

CAN Orwell crack the secret to controlling Alias?

Find out in the final episode of Golem:
Alias

Turn the page to read Chapter 1...

Safe and Sound?

Nadia had four little humans on her hands and twenty minutes to leave the bunker. Twenty minutes to game over. Aisha, Majid, Samir and Sebastian wouldn't get a second chance. They were twelve and thirteen years old. They'd only ever known one set of graphics: the tower blocks of the Moreland Estate. If they weren't out of B Corp HQ in twenty minutes, they'd be stuck on level one for ever. Grey sky. Cold concrete.

And Nadia had run out of ideas.

The route she'd thought was etched in her memory had disappeared. She remembered the cries of horror, the gaping wounds, the terror-filled eyes. She could still see the splayed corpses, right there, in front of her.

"Miss?" Aisha asked. "Are they dead?"

Yes. They were dead. But Nadia no longer knew in what order they'd died. And right now, to get out of this maze, she needed to know. They had to get from bloodbath number 5 back to bloodbath number 4 and so on, until they reached what was left of the big glass door at the main entrance.

Corridors, halls, security doors, stairs … Nadia didn't recognize anything any more. She'd followed Natasha, panic-stricken and terrified. Now she had to take the same path, but in the opposite direction. On her own. Correction: with four children. And she'd never seen them like this before. Mute.

"Childwen, I think…"

Don't cry. Make a decision. Hadn't she already followed these red lines on the floor? Yes, but which way? Her eyes met Majid's. The kid was begging her to do something, to know the answer. He's counting on me, thought Nadia, he's counting on me so badly.

"Over there."

When she saw the glass doors with ghostly computers lined up behind them in the gloom, she knew she'd gone the wrong way. But she carried on. Nothing else for it.

Twenty minutes, Natasha had said. How much time was left? She didn't want to look at her watch. They'd just reached a huge open space, a chilled zone where hundreds of packages were stacked up. A dispatch warehouse. She definitely hadn't come this way.

"Childwen, I'm not sure…" She glanced desperately back down the long corridor. She had to make a decision. Fast.

"I've made a mistake. We've got to turn back. We're going to have to run fast, OK?"

But the children weren't listening. They didn't trust her any more.

"The truck!" Sebastian shouted. He climbed up into a forklift truck and frantically tried the controls.

"Leave it," said Samir. Shoving his friend out of the way, he got in the driver's seat and managed to start the engine. "Get in, everybody!"

They hurtled along for two hundred metres,

past walls of piled-up boxes. The underground warehouse seemed to go on and on. Nadia was standing on the platform at the back of the truck, clinging to Aisha as she peered into the darkness ahead. That's not the exit, she thought. Suddenly she saw a sign hanging from a chain. She recognized the stylized image of a forklift truck.

It was crossed out with a big red line.

"Thamir! Not that way! It's not allowed!"

"'Low it, man."

The truck and its five passengers tipped down onto a ramp. Slowly, ever so slowly, it picked up speed.

Samir clung to the steering wheel, and made it round the first two bends without mishap. Then the truck scraped against the wall. And suddenly smashed into it: once, twice. A third bump, more violent than the others, bounced it back towards the opposite wall, flinging out its passengers.

Nadia was the last to get up, rubbing her sore elbow. "Are you all wight, childwen?"

But they'd gone on without her, sliding down the ramp as if she was no longer part of the group. They fell over. They got up again. Nobody cried out. By the time she caught up, they'd reached an underground car park.

"It's the right one," Sebastian called out. He'd recognized his parents' camper van. No matter how big the car park, the Volkswagen was always easy to spot.

The keys were on the dashboard. As they headed out, all the barriers were raised, all doors open. Here, like everywhere else, Alias had unlocked everything.

The camper van exited the mountainside the way it had entered: by the north entrance. It emerged into moonlight on a section of road two hundred metres long.

The blast from the explosion was so powerful, Nadia momentarily lost control of the wheel. It was like the camper van wasn't on the road any more. Like it was flying. She couldn't see anything. Just a few reflections in the windscreen, a few snatched images in the rear-view mirror. A ball of fire. A giant shadow. The top part of the bunker lifting off like a saucepan lid, before crashing back down again.

Crushing everything.

She spared a thought for those still inside. Albert? Natasha? Hugh?

Nadia put her foot on the accelerator and shot down the deserted road. A few minutes later, she slammed on the brakes. There were two cars blocking the way. Police! About time. She couldn't keep this up much longer.

"We're saved!"

Three policemen made their way over, training their torches on the VW. Nadia saw the face of one of them pressed against the window. Then she couldn't see anything: he was blinding her with the light.

"I've got the childwen with me," she said through the lowered window. "Safe and sound."

The door opened. Nadia started to climb out. But a hand grabbed her arm and wrenched her from the driver's seat. She screamed. The policeman twisted her arm behind her back and flung her against the side of the VW. Her forehead hit the bodywork. She could feel hands all over her, on her sides, her stomach, her thighs. All three of them had surrounded her. One yanked her hair to make her turn her head. Torches were sweeping up and down her.

A man spoke. "It's her. It's Michelle."

She recognized that voice. Stefano! The playboy with the red convertible.

"The children! Get the children out!" somebody yelled.

Nadia was driven to Gruyères police station. She was taken into a room with bars on the window. Just like that. No explanation. Stunned, she collapsed on a chair. It felt like her day had started forty hours ago…

Somebody shook her roughly. "What is it? The weapon – what kind is it?"

The remains of a dream were still floating before her eyes. She was caught under the smoking rubble of a warehouse ravaged by fire. Nadia had never fallen asleep sitting on a chair before.

"They say it makes holes that won't close up again," said the man who was leaning over her. He shook her again and repeated his question. Urgently. "What is it?"

Nadia could feel the blood pounding in her head. In the muffled world where she was struggling, nothing seemed very urgent.

Then the man asked her something odd. "What organization do you belong to?"

She looked at him wearily. Only one thing mattered. "Where are the childwen?" she asked.

"They're safe."

Something wasn't right. Nadia could tell. From the way they were treating her, from the way this man was talking to her. But she was too exhausted to put up a fight.

"I'm not planning on conducting a full interrogation for the time being," said the man. "You know what interests me."

Nadia shook her head.

"Are we still in danger?" he asked. "More bombs?"

She shuddered. "Please," she whispered, "I want to go home."

The man was surprised. He sat down opposite her, his hands on his knees. "I'm Eberhardt," he said. "Michelle isn't your real name, is it?"

"No. It's Nadia Martin."

"There's something I simply don't understand. Why did you and your fellow terrorist hitch a lift?"

Nadia felt her body temperature drop several degrees. Her fellow terrorist?

"I mean, you already had a vehicle. That camper van's yours, isn't it?"

She nodded, then confessed, "Well, no, actually, it belongs to Sebathian's dad. Sebathian's one of the childwen."

This information confused Eberhardt even more. "Is he part of the network?"

"What network?"

Thinking Eberhardt was about to hit her, Nadia covered her face. Fortunately, his attention was diverted as the door opened and another man came in.

"Drop it," said the newcomer. "We've got the first autopsy report. This one's not for us." And then he added scornfully, "They're bringing in the BIB boys." He nodded in Nadia's direction. "She's to go into solitary. No more questions."

Nadia wondered if this was good news.

She lay down on the mattress in the cell and slept right through till the following day. At least, that was what she thought. But when she saw three meal trays that nobody had cleared away still on the floor, she realized she must have slept for longer.

Everything was cold. She swallowed a few mouthfuls of rice and emptied three beakers of water, one after the other.

An hour later, she met the BIB boys.

Tommy was Afro-Caribbean. Payne was blond. They were waiting for her in a comfortable room, without any bars on the window. They'd had their food trays too. There were leftover hamburgers and large Big B cola cans on the table. Tommy and Payne had travelled a long way, and it showed: crumpled faces, rumpled clothes.

"We work for the Big Investigation Bureau," announced Payne. "We were notified" – he looked at his watch – "fourteen hours ago. And here we are." He looked chuffed. He was perched on the edge of the table, his bottom framed by junk food. "As I'm sure you'll appreciate, we don't get called out for run-of-the-mill terrorism cases."

"We're here because of what we're about to show you," said Tommy, closing the blinds.

On the table, in the middle of all the discarded

packaging, was an old-fashioned slide projector. When Payne shone the first image onto the small wall screen, Nadia looked away. It showed the lifeless bodies of the B Corp cowboys slaughtered in the B Happy Land car park. The photos that followed were close-ups.

Tommy was standing next to the screen, with a pointer. "The projectile entered here, piercing the cheek, or malar bone, and severing the pterygoid muscles before exiting at the back of the skull, at the level of the petro-occipital suture, after causing exactly the sort of damage you would expect to the cerebral matter."

Nadia tried not to hiccup.

"There's a small incision at the entrance to these wounds – a very clean incision."

"Surgical," Payne added.

Click. Another image appeared on the screen. Another wound. Another trajectory.

"Not a drop of blood in those wounds," Tommy pointed out. "The projectile tunnels into the flesh like a drill. But a human head isn't a plank of wood. What we're seeing here, Miss Martin, is, by definition, impossible."

They both turned to face Nadia.

"The weapon isn't one we're familiar with," said Tommy.

"Although there are some similarities with the Annapolis affair in Maryland," Payne concluded.

"May 1990. A case that was never solved."

"Miss Martin," said Payne, "what *is* this weapon? Where does it come from?"

Nadia took a deep breath. And provided the only information she could. "An ewaser-laser."

Tommy nodded. "We were thinking along those lines."

"Were you acting under duress?" asked Payne.

Nadia widened her scared eyes and nodded. She'd have to play it very carefully. "That ... cweature is tewifying."

"What d'you know about her?" asked Tommy.

"She says her name's Natatha. But I don't think she's totally human."

The men glanced at each other. Clearly they'd already reached this conclusion.

"You're the only witness to what happened in the building," Tommy went on. "There were twenty-eight fatalities."

Nadia had one burning question, but she held back. She would have given anything to find out whether the fatalities included a tall muscly man with brown hair, and an overgrown teenager with an old-fashioned name… No, actually she'd rather not know.

"I've forgotten nearly everything," she whispered, trying her best to sound convincing. "I was totally under the contwol of that cweature. I just acted like a wobot. I can wemember scweaming, flashes of light, smoke … and then … and then … I found the childwen. My students." She started sobbing, without having to try too hard.

Just then there was a knock at the door. It was Eberhardt. "We've got proof," he said, holding out a sheet of paper. "She's a terrorist based in Moreland Town."

"Yeah," said Payne absent-mindedly. He took the piece of paper and shooed Eberhardt away. He glanced at it, then turned back to Nadia. "The police have searched your home, Miss Martin. They found dangerous chemicals in your kitchen."

The ingredients Nadia had used to make tear-gas.

"I'm a science teacher. They're chemicals for my expewiments—"

"There's no need to justify yourself, Miss Martin," interrupted Tommy. "Where we come from, most teachers prefer to go to school armed."

"You've had a big shock," said Payne, putting a friendly hand on her shoulder. "You need to rest up. And we're going to do all we can to track down this creature before…" There was a lump in his throat. He carried on huskily. "Before she puts our whole civilization at risk."

"Payne gets very emotional," explained Tommy. "He can go a bit over the top." He looked at his watch. "We're going to have to break off this interview. We've asked to attend the autopsy of one of the victims. There's a lot at stake here."

"Are they going to keep me in pwison?"

"It's not for us to decide," Payne replied. "But we're going to send you a Red Cross volunteer who'll be a great comfort to you."

"Miss Goody."

"Yes, Miss Goody," echoed Payne, as if her name alone was a great comfort.